IN A SPLIT SECOND

TIMOTHY GLASS

Platinum Paw Press

CONTENTS

In a Split
Second

In a Spilt Second

Written by Timothy Glass

Copyright (C) 2018

Cover art by Timothy Glass

Library of Congress Control Number 2018955675

ISBN number 978-0-9984121-9-1

DEDICATION

To my mentor, director/producer Paul Gray. I was both fortunate and blessed that our paths crossed. Your direction, education, and friendship in my career and in my life are so appreciated. Thank you until we meet again.

Also, to one of the most prolific businessmen of our times, Dan Valente: You were an inspiration to me and to others. You will be dearly missed.

ACKNOWLEDGMENTS

As always, thank you to my wife, Cathy, for putting up with the countless hours I spent clicking away on the keyboard and for your support and understanding of what I do.

To my wonderful fans, who encourage me to keep going when things get tough and who always look forward to what I have coming out next.

To all the men and women who spend countless hours putting their lives on the line. In many situations, it is a thankless job.

To my favorite Starbucks team at store #47714 for providing me with the fuel to keep going and for your wonderful service. Thank you.

The bitterest tears shed over graves are for words
left unsaid and deeds left undone.
~Harriet Beecher Stowe

INTRODUCTION

A red glow from the gun's laser sight danced across
the pillow, casting an eerie image and creating a
stark contrast to the dark, moonless night. With
precision, the red laser dot stopped and zeroed in on
the forehead of Bud Hampton as he lay peaceful
and still, sleeping in his bed. For a split second, the
laser dot held a steady position. The intruder never
wavered or had a second thought. Long before this
night, he had made up his mind about what he
would do. He carefully squeezed the trigger and felt
the first recoil of the Glock 9mm. Another deep
breath steadied his aim and he squeezed off a
second round. The gun's silencer created two
muffled sounds in quick succession. These were

followed by a woman's scream, which echoed in the darkness.

As planned, he quickly left the room. He was out the back door and into the darkness without another thought about the victim who now lay dead. He was glad he had shot out the streetlight several hours earlier. Dressed entirely in black, he knew no one would be able to detect his movements. He sprinted over a fence and into the neighbor's yard, then out into the street. He continued running two streets down to his parked car. With the dome light off, he opened the door and entered the vehicle, then removed the ski mask, the black gloves, and, lastly, the paper booties he had worn over his shoes. He smiled, remembering how he had thought to spray paint the shoe covers black weeks before. That way, not even a footprint would be left behind in the house or outside it.

He inserted the key in the ignition. As the engine came to life, he pulled away from the curb. Once he reached the intersection one block west, he turned on the headlights. He looked in the rearview mirror, his emotions as blank as the road he left behind.

CHAPTER 1

*L*akewood was a suburb of the big city of Petersburg, thirty minutes north of Tuckersville. Nestled below the mountains, the town was located in a valley rich in farmland and hardworking families.

As daylight gave way to night, darkness rolled through Lakewood like a tsunami. Porch lights pierced the darkness. The evening air was filled with the aroma of home-cooked dinners and fireplace smoke. The hands of time ticked on. In the moonless night, window curtains were pulled shut, signaling the end of the day as people retired to their bedrooms. Windows that had radiated warm lamplight were now darkened as the night grew cooler and stillness settled over the town.

"911, what's your emergency?"

"My…boyfriend, ah…he's been shot!"

"May I have your name?"

"Ellie…Ellie Peters."

Ellie was still stunned as the tan telephone cord shook in the air. No matter what she did, she couldn't stop her hands – much less the rest of her body – from shaking. Her mind was still trying to process what had just happened.

"Give me your address, please," the dispatcher requested.

"Ah…7 Woodlark Road."

"Is your boyfriend still breathing?"

"No…no, he's been shot."

"Yes, I know, but is he breathing?"

"No, he's gone…he's dead."

"Is the person who shot your boyfriend still in the house now?"

"No, I saw him running out the back door."

"Do you know the person who shot your boyfriend?"

"No…all I could see was his back. All his clothes were black."

"You said *him*, *he*, and *his*, so you know the person was a male?"

"No…but it looked like a male. He was tall, about six feet."

"I've dispatched officers to the house. Stay on the phone with me. I won't hang up until the officers get there. Is anyone else in the house with you?"

"My daughter."

"Is she okay?"

"Yes, we're both in the living room right now."

"What's her name?"

"Kim…Peters."

In the distance, Ellie heard a police siren. She hoped – no, prayed – the cops would get there soon.

"Ms. Peters, talk to me so I know you're alright."

"I'm okay. I can hear the sirens."

"The officers should be there in about three minutes or so."

CHAPTER 2

*D*etective Connor Maxwell's phone rang just after 3 a.m. Reaching across his partner for his phone on the nightstand, he knew the only one calling at this hour had to be the dispatcher with the Lakewood Police Department.

Connor Maxwell was the envy of the department. Not because he had made detective; no, it was because of his partner, a snappy, petite redhead. She was bright and could outrun almost any of the cops, including Connor. Unlike any other partner with whom Connor had toured, she knew her job well and took it seriously. She never tried to pull rank or grandstand like some of the cops with whom Connor had worked during his ten years with the department. His partner's name was Sundae, and she had a sweet disposition to match her unique personality.

Sundae and Connor had lived together for a little over five years. Their relationship was still as strong and trusting as it had been when they first met. One might say that Sundae had a nose for solving crime. Everyone said she had a wiggle when she walked, which attracted stares when she and Connor walked into the police department. Together, they made a great partnership. Sundae did stick her nose into things, though most of the time this trait helped them solve the crimes they investigated. Other times, Sundae got herself into messes. Then again, that was par for the course, even for a seasoned officer like Sundae. The fact was, Sundae was a canine – a 13-inch beagle, to be exact.

CHAPTER 3

Deputy David Smith of the Natick
Sheriff's Department drove slowly
eastward on the old two-lane highway leading
toward the outskirts of Lakewood. David blinked
several times, trying to adjust his eyes from the well-
lit streets of Lakewood to the solitary reflection of
the white and yellow lines that ran down the center
of the road on the outskirts of town. This stretch of
State Highway 10 was in dire need of re-paving, or
at least resurfacing, he thought to himself.
Nonetheless, this being a state highway, that decision
was up to the state, not the town.

About five minutes after his unit rolled down
State Highway 10, David saw what looked like fresh
skid marks leading off the highway.

The tracks entered the dense brush and trees; whatever made them had crushed the leaves, branches, and bushes in its path. 'What was it?' David thought as he hit the brakes, maneuvering a U-turn back to the skid marks. With his spotlight, he scanned the marks and beyond to the brush and trees, but saw nothing. It was Christmas break and the kids were out of school. Had someone been going too fast and not seen the yellow sign warning them about a curve in the highway ahead? Worse, could one of the kids on break have had a few drinks?

David pulled over his police unit. "21, SO I'll be 10-6 at mile marker 12 on State Highway 10."

He reached for the door handle. However, before he could get out of the patrol car, David saw, in his rearview mirror, a shadowy figure step out from behind a bush on the side of the highway opposite the skid marks.

David turned the spotlight toward the figure approaching his patrol car and stepped out. He could see that this was no teenager; it was a young man in his late twenties or early thirties.

David trained his flashlight on the man's face just as another Sheriff's Department unit rolled up behind him. It was Officer Dan Keller.

"I missed the curve." The young man pointed toward the skid marks.

"I can see that," David said.

Keeping his flashlight on the man, David looked over his body. The young man's eyes weren't bloodshot. David made a mental note that no blood or scratches were apparent on the man's body. He noted that the man wore blue jeans, a white T-shirt, and slip-on shoes.

"You okay?" Deputy Smith inquired.

"Yeah, I'm fine. A little shook up, that's all."

"I need to see your driver's license, insurance card, and registration, please," David said.

The young man pulled out his wallet and handed his license to David, who looked it over as the other deputy stood at his side.

"Wait here," David said as he left the deputy and the young man where they stood. After returning to his patrol car, he entered the man's ID in the NCIC database. There were no outstanding warrants. David exited his patrol car.

"I was telling the officer that my registration and insurance card are in the glove box. I'll go get them." The young man quickly turned.

"We'll go down there with you." The brush was well over their heads in some areas as the three men descended, weaving their way toward the disabled car. Once they reached it, David saw that the car wasn't drivable.

Keller unclipped his mic. "29 SO, I need a wrecker on State Highway 10. We're about a mile outside Lakewood."

The young man quickly reached inside the glove box for his insurance card and registration. David handed the documents to Dan, who radioed the Sheriff's Department dispatcher and asked that she run a check on the car. Then the three men walked back up to the highway.

"Any alcohol this evening?" David asked, looking again at the young man's eyes.

"No, nothing at all."

David noted that the man's breath didn't smell of alcohol. When he had briefly looked over the car, he had seen neither bottles nor drug paraphernalia. Once back at his patrol car, David gave the man a field sobriety test, which he passed.

"I told you, I just missed the curve. I usually don't drive this stretch of road but it was late and this was a shortcut."

"Do you have anyone we could call to pick you up?"

"No. Would you please call me a cab to take me home?"

David wrote a few notes, then looked up. "Just one more thing. Your car was on the east side of the road. Why, then, did you approach my car from the west side of the highway?"

"I had to take a leak…I was afraid to stay too close to the car in case the gas tank burst into flames."

CHAPTER 4

The still hours between midnight and 4 a.m. were dark, damp, and cold. The month of December had been unseasonably frigid that year. From the open window, Connor felt dampness on the stubble of his left cheek as he slowly drove several streets down from the crime scene. He hadn't bothered to shave when he got the call; he just put on his jeans, a V-neck sweater, a sport coat, and his boots – or as his co-workers called them, his Oki-Air's. He had run his comb through his unruly, thick, dark brown hair.

Most neighborhoods even he wouldn't go into at this hour, but in his profession, one had no choice. Connor felt the pressure on his lower back from the Glock 9mm inside the pancake holster on his belt.

This was a nice neighborhood; still, he listened for dogs barking or any odd noise. Glancing from side to side, he watched for a person who fit the description that dispatch had given him. Driving several streets down and around the crime scene was a habit of his, one that gave him a feel for the neighborhood. It was a habit for which some of his co-workers criticized him behind his back. Get to the crime scene as soon as possible, with sirens blaring – that was their approach. Connor knew the uniformed officers on duty that night were seasoned, well-trained officers who would separate any witnesses and secure the crime scene.

He made mental notes as he drove through the streets. Middle-class neighborhood, well-kept yards. The type of neighborhood where dreams of owning a home and raising a family were made reality. Nothing stood out, no one yelling or screaming. No doors slamming and no one under a streetlight making a drug connection, even at this hour of the early morning. In some neighborhoods on the edge of Lakewood, this type of behavior was common. However, this neighborhood wasn't one of those places. Why, then, Connor thought to himself, would a young man sleeping in his own bed be murdered?

Sundae put her front paws on the window, peering out of the unit. Connor rolled to a stop at 7 Woodlark Road. Sundae knew she was to stay in the car until Connor commanded her to jump out or until she felt his life was in danger; then she would leave to protect him. Grabbing a pair of latex gloves and paper shoe covers from the glove box, Connor walked toward the uniformed officer.

"The vic is dead, sir. No pulse," McHenry said to Connor. "Dispatch has already called the ME. The vic's name is Bud Hampton, according to the girlfriend and his driver's license. Thirty-five years old."

"Thanks." Connor quickly walked toward the front door. McHenry ran up to his side.

"Detective, the girlfriend said there was a black backpack on the den floor that doesn't belong to the vic, her, or her daughter."

"Thanks. I'll have the CI team check it out."

Connor entered, then turned back to McHenry.

"Where are the girlfriend and her daughter?"

"Transported by separate units to the PD. Detective Stroup will meet them there. They left a few minutes before you got here, sir. PD will put them into separate holding rooms until you get there."

Once inside, Connor looked around the living room. Nothing really looked out of place. A cordless phone was off the charger, lying on the couch. Connor thought to himself that it had probably been left there after the girlfriend called 911.

In the master bedroom, everything seemed to be in its proper place, like something out of Good Housekeeping magazine...if only a body wasn't lying dead in the bed, his eyes staring vacantly at the ceiling.

Conner knew every crime had a story. He stood beside the victim and looked down at him. What could have led up to someone wanting this man dead? Was the girlfriend mad because she'd found him with another woman? If only the dead could talk. If only Connor had a nickel for every time he'd wished that; he would be retired now and living on the beach in Hawaii.

Connor lifted the blankets and saw that blood had pooled in the back and buttocks area. This meant the body had not been moved. He then looked under the bed. Nothing.

"We really need to stop meeting this way."

From behind him, Connor heard a deep, gruff voice. He looked toward the doorway. It was Malcolm Greenblatt, ME, his large frame filling the doorway. Connor always thought that no matter what time of day or night he ran into Malcolm, his clothes looked like the sheets on an unmade bed. Malcolm's shirt was buttoned but gaped open, exposing his belly button.

"So, what do we have here?" Malcolm asked.

"Bud Hampton, age 35, single. Girlfriend told dispatch they were asleep in their bed when a perp came in and shot him, then went out the back door."

"Shot, I'll buy," Malcolm said as he put his hand on Bud's neck, checking for a pulse. Malcolm pulled back the covers and looked over the body. He then got his stethoscope out of his bag and listened for a heartbeat.

Connor wrote some notes in his book: "Judging by the residue on his forehead and the blood spatter on the wall, he was shot at close range."

"Did he upset the girlfriend?" Malcolm asked.

"Not sure what happened. Only time will tell."

CHAPTER 5

The police department was a zoo that night. Connor gave a friendly smile to the female dispatcher as he entered with Sundae at his side and weaved his way through uniformed officers and perps.

"I thought this happened only on full moons," Connor said.

"Apparently not," the dispatcher said.

"Listen, if any of the uniforms pick up a guy dressed all in black, about six feet tall, let me know as soon as possible."

Connor walked down the hallway and stopped in front of a large window. Watching through the one-way glass, he observed Ellie Peters. She sat calmly, waiting. Too calmly, he thought, for a woman who had just lost her boyfriend. Once he entered, Connor walked over to the chair across the table from her.

"Ms. Peters, my name is Detective Connor Maxwell and this is my partner, Sundae. I hope you don't mind a canine in the room."

"No, not at all." She reached out to Sundae, who sniffed Ellie's hand and then sat next to Connor, watching her.

"I'll be recording this interview," Connor said, pressing the start button on the machine on the table. For several seconds, Ellie's gaze fell on the red light on the machine in front of her.

"Detective, where is my daughter?"

"She's with Detective Kate Stroup right down the hallway."

"I don't know why she can't be here with me."

Connor watched Ellie's hand and facial expressions.

"Could you state your full name, please?"

"Yes, Ellie Peters."

"Ms. or Mrs.?"

"Ms."

"Ms. Peters, I'm sorry for your loss."

Connor waited for Ellie to say something but there was no response.

"Were you in a relationship with Mr. Hampton?"

"We lived together, if that's what you're asking."

"As a couple or just roommates?"

"No, we were a couple."

"How long had you been living with Mr. Hampton?"

"A couple of months."

Connor noticed she used the proper syntax. When asked the question, many people who had just lost a loved one said "we are" a couple, not "we were." Connor wrote a notation in his book.

"And the young girl, Kim, is she your daughter or Mr. Hampton's?"

"No, Kim is my daughter."

As she talked, Connor jotted notes in his book.

"So Kim is from a previous relationship?"

"Yes, I was married before and we are divorced."

"So, your ex-husband is Kim's father?"

"Yes, we divorced about a year ago."

"And do you share custody with your ex-husband? I don't believe you said his name."

"Sam Peters. We share joint custody of our daughter."

Sundae walked over to Ellie, who reached down

to pet her. Connor knew that Sundae was at work, too, sniffing Ellie's hand and pant legs. He watched, as Sundae seemed to relieve some of the tension in the room.

"Would you say the breakup was…"

"We both no longer wanted the marriage."

"How old did you say Kim was?"

"Twelve."

"How does your ex-husband like your present living situation?"

"We talked about it before I moved in with Bud. He seemed okay with it."

"And your daughter, how did she get along with Mr. Hampton?"

"Ah…well, I guess she'd rather have her father and I back together… but…" Ellie looked at the floor. Connor watched her body language. "I think she knows that's never going to happen."

"Is Mr. Peters seeing someone now?"

"Detective, he was before the divorce."

"So would it be safe to say that your daughter may not be happy with your living with Mr. Hampton?"

"Detective, what does any of this have to do with what happened tonight?"

"Will you excuse me? I'll be back shortly. Can I get you anything?"

"Water would be nice."

Connor left the room, Sundae trailing closely behind him. They walked down the hallway. Connor knocked on a door several rooms down from where Ellie sat. Kim was with a man whom Connor didn't know. Detective Kate Stoup stepped into the hallway and closed the door behind her.

"Who's the guy?" Connor asked.

"Her dad."

Connor was well aware that to talk to a juvie, they had to have either a parent or an attorney present.

"What do we have?" Connor asked.

"The father is clearly upset. He wants to take the daughter home. The daughter is 12 years old. She said she was asleep until she heard her mother scream." Detective Stroup bent down to pet Sundae, who wagged her tail while looking up at Kate.

"Kim stated she stayed in her room until her mother came to get her," Detective Stroup continued.

"Her mother told me she wasn't a happy camper about her mother living with the vic. Said she wanted her mother and father to get back together."

Kate smiled at Connor. "So does every little boy or girl of divorced parents across America."

"Any emotional expression from the child regarding what happened tonight?"

Detective Stroup shook her head no. "Any from the mother?" she asked.

"No, calm. Too calm. Oh, and McHenry told me there was a backpack left in the den that didn't belong to either the mother or daughter. Did the child mention that?"

"No."

"I have the CSI team looking at the scene. Maybe something will come of that."

"What did the house look like?" Detective Stroup asked.

"Clean. Almost too clean."

"Did the child have any blood on her?"

"None."

"The mother?" Detective Stroup asked.

"Not a drop and says she was lying right next to our vic in bed. I better get back to her."

"Listen, if it's okay with you, I'm going to cut the daughter loose and let the father take her home. If we don't, I think he'll lawyer up. He's pretty pissed at this point. I have all his contact info. I'll be in to listen to the girlfriend in a few."

Connor stopped outside the room and once again watched Ellie sitting there. Within inches of her hand was a box of tissues, which she hadn't yet touched. Odd, he thought to himself.

"Let's go back inside, Sundae."

Sundae, wagging her tail, followed Connor back into the room. He handed a water bottle to Ellie.

"Ellie, can you think of anyone who would want to hurt Bud?"

"No."

"Did you and Bud ever do drugs?"

"Oh, God no!"

"Did Bud gamble, hang around with anyone… who didn't seem like they were on the up and up?"

Ellie hesitated. "No, not that I'm aware of."

"Was Bud married before, or did he have any ex-girlfriends?"

"He was never married. To my knowledge he didn't have any long-term relationships until me."

"How was your relationship with Bud?"

"We were planning to get married, we just hadn't told anyone yet," Ellie said.

"Getting married, that can be stressful," Connor said.

He leaned back in the chair and tapped his pen on the pad, studying her reaction and body language.

"Not really. We felt it was the natural next step," Ellie replied.

"What about you? I know you said you were married. Was Bud the first person you dated after your marriage broke up?"

"No. I had a relationship with one guy and moved in with him."

"How long did that last?"

"About three months and we broke it off." Connor waited to see if she would volunteer anything more.

"Can you tell me what his name is?"

"Brad...Hopper. There was another guy. We went out on maybe...three dates, but I never returned his calls after I met Bud."

"What was his name?"

"Jeff, let me think, ...Gilbert, that's it. Jeff Gilbert."

CHAPTER 6

The day after the murder, as he entered the backyard, Connor retraced the killer's path at 7 Woodlark as Ellie had described it to him. Sundae kept sniffing the living room carpet where the black backpack had once laid. Kate carefully looked over the bedroom in case something had been missed. The three of them met in the backyard.

Connor motioned for Sundae to do a sweep of the backyard. Sundae quickly crisscrossed the yard, sniffing every step of the way.

"I'm going next door to talk to the neighbor. I saw her unloading groceries a few minutes ago," Kate said.

Connor watched Sundae for any sign that the

beagle had found something. Several minutes later, Connor called Sundae. He locked up the house and put her into his unmarked patrol unit. Then he joined Kate next door.

As he approached the front door, he saw the elderly, silver-haired homeowner in a blue chair, talking to Kate. The elderly woman motioned for him to come in through the glass storm door.

"Why, I thought you'd bring that cute little puppy over. I had a beagle when I was a child. Wonderful pets," she said with a smile. She paused, reminiscing.

"Hi, I'm Detective Connor Maxwell."

"Such a sad thing that happened to Mr. Hampton, such a nice man he was. He helped me put up new rain gutters last summer. I have a handyman coming over today to install safety locks on all my doors and an alarm system by the end of the week."

"Mrs. Wilson, have you ever met Mr. Hampton's girlfriend?" Kate asked.

"Why yes, I had them over several times for dinner. Nice couple."

"Did you ever hear them fighting or yelling?"

Mrs. Wilson thought for a moment, then shook her head no.

"Did you ever notice anything odd at their house, say, cars coming at all times of the day or night?"

"Why, no. Both of them worked and left early in the morning, then returned around six when I watch the news."

"Did you hear or see anything last night?" Connor asked.

Mrs. Wilson pointed toward Hampton's house. "I did notice our street light was out. The city had just replaced it about two weeks ago."

Connor stood and handed a business card to Mrs. Wilson. Kate did the same.

"If you think of anything else, please give us a call."

Kate and Connor said nothing until they were in the police unit.

"Any thoughts yet?" Connor asked as he pulled away from the curb and headed downtown.

"Let's grab some lunch and then pay a visit to her ex-boyfriend. Maybe they decided to rekindle the fire and Bud was in their way."

Kate sat on one side of the booth, while Connor and Sundae sat on the other. The owners of the café had no problem allowing Sundae into their establishment. As the owner always said, Sundae served her community and was always a quiet customer – unlike some.

"I almost forgot to tell you that the reporter from the Morning Times called wanting a statement about last night's homicide. I tried to give her one but she wanted to talk to you." Kate smiled at Connor. "I think she just wanted to talk to you."

Connor set down his menu and looked at Kate. "She asked me out the other night."

"And?"

"I'd rather sit on I-95 during rush hour with a sign that says 'hit me.'"

"Connor, not every woman is like your ex-wife."

A young woman sat behind the walnut desk.

"I'd like to speak to Mr. Brad Hopper, please," Connor said.

"I'm sorry but Mr. Hopper is with a client right now and can't be disturbed."

Connor reached for his badge under his sport coat and showed it to the woman behind the desk.

"I'm Detective Connor Maxwell and this is Detective Kate Stroup. We need to talk to Mr. Hopper right now."

The woman quickly picked up the phone and dialed.

"Mr. Hopper, two detectives are out here. They say they need to talk to you."

She set the phone back on the cradle. "Mr. Hopper will be right out. If you wish, you can take a seat over there by the window."

Before Connor and Kate sat down, Brad Hopper entered the lobby. Connor noted that he was about six feet tall, with an athletic build and dressed in a suit and tie.

"I'm Brad Hopper," he said, his hand extended to shake hands with both of them.

"Is there somewhere a little more private where we can talk?" Connor asked him.

"Yes, of course. Why don't we step into my office?"

Connor and Kate followed Brad down the hallway and into an office. Brad shut the door behind them, then took a seat behind his desk.

"How can I help you, detectives?"

Kate took a seat as Connor looked over the framed diplomas on Brad's wall.

"Harvard. I'm impressed," Connor said as he sat next to Kate.

Brad smiled and looked at Connor. "Thank you, but I'm sure you're not here to discuss my degrees."

"Mr. Hopper..."

"Please, call me Brad."

"Brad, do you know Ellie Peters?"

Brad hesitated.

CHAPTER 7

Kate scanned the computer screen on her desk. The clicking sounds from the keyboard suddenly stopped as her hands hovered over the keys. Connor glanced across his desk in her direction.

"Got something?"

"Mr. Hopper said he had never owned a gun. But I found that he purchased a gun about six years ago."

"What caliber?"

Kate looked at the screen. "It was a rifle." She shrugged. "Could he have forgotten?"

"Or lied." Connor smiled.

"You know that old saying: Words are silver but silence is golden."

Connor thought about what Kate had said. Brad Hopper could have omitted the fact that he had once purchased a gun.

Kate came over and leaned on the side of Connor's desk. "He stated that he and Ellie broke up and remained friends."

Connor chuckled. "Kate, not every guy is a dirt bag like your ex-husband."

"Don't remind me."

Connor stood and walked over to an old gray steel filing cabinet, where he put the file in the top drawer marked "active".

"Kate, Brad was on a business trip. The hotel has already confirmed he was hundreds of miles away on the night of the murder."

Kate turned toward Connor. "What if he hired someone to get rid of Bud?"

"Anything is possible, but it seems to me he has moved on from their relationship. He has a girlfriend and he said they're engaged. To me, that says he has moved on, or did you forget?"

"You're right," Kate said, looking back to a file on her desk.

Connor walked to the whiteboard. With his back turned to Kate, he studied its contents, which resembled a family tree of sorts. First was a photo of

Bud Hampton, the victim. From there, the tree branched off to Ellie Peters, the girlfriend. Another branch, with a red marker, led to her daughter, Kim Peters. The last branch on that side came to Sam Peters, Ellie's ex- husband. Below the victim's photo were the only two other branches. One contained a photo of Brad Hopper, while the other was a photo of Jeff Gilbert. Ellie had given both photos to Connor.

"I wonder about the girlfriend or even the 12-year-old daughter." Connor turned and looked at Kate.

"The CSI team turned the house upside down. There wasn't so much as a toy gun," Kate said over background noise of ringing phones.

"What if it was…" Connor turned back to the whiteboard and pointed at the photo of Sam Peters. "The ex-husband. You said he was pissed off." Connor turned back to Kate.

"Connor, I think you'd be pissed off if your little girl was woken up in the middle of the night by her mother screaming and her mother's boyfriend dead in his bed."

"You have to admit, the little girl could have let her father in the house to hide in her bedroom until the deed was done. The little girl gets her family back, the ex gets his wife back, and our vic is out of the way."

"Connor, my gut tells me the little girl had nothing to do with it, nor did her dad."

Kate reached down to pet Sundae, whose head was in Kate's desk drawer. From it, Sundae quickly grabbed a box of cheese snacks.

"Sundae, I wish you'd help us find the killer instead of all my treats."

"We still have the girlfriend," Connor said as he walked back to his desk. He grabbed his sport coat off the back of his chair and his car keys off the desk. At the sound of the keys jingling, Sundae wagged her tail. "Let's call it a day. Maybe tomorrow we can talk to the other ex-boyfriend."

Connor walked around their desks and took the box of cheese treats from Sundae. He handed them to Kate before heading toward the door.

"Too bad we're not looking for a food bandit," Kate said, petting Sundae, who got up and quickly followed Connor. "Don't forget, you need to call that reporter from the Morning Times."

From the doorway, Connor waved as if dismissing what she had just said about the reporter.

After Kate watched Connor and Sundae leave, she peered into the bottom of the desk drawer. She removed a yellow tablet from the bottom and stared at a photo of herself in a wedding dress and her ex-husband in a tux. She pulled the photo from the drawer and held it over her trashcan.

"File this under happier times," she whispered.

Kate watched the photo spin and slowly drop into the trashcan. Deep in thought, she remembered that things had been great between them…until she graduated from the academy. Her long hours, weekends, nights, and overtime had quickly taken their toll…as had the other woman with whom Kate had later found her husband. Plus, there were the comments he had made shortly after she graduated from the academy – comments about hating the fact that she was a cop.

Eventually, they both found that friendly get-togethers with long-time friends were no longer fun. Kate blamed herself. She could no longer relate to their friends, especially the females. They talked about their days at work, business meetings, and lunches. It all seemed mundane when Kate spent her days meeting people at their worst. How on earth could one compare their nine-to-five office jobs to chasing a punk through the streets? Added to the equation was the fact that many of the things Kate did for work were confidential. She simply couldn't discuss them with anyone but another officer.

A fight in the booking room across the hall interrupted her thoughts of the past. Kate straightened up her desk for the night, locked her files in the filing cabinet, and headed for the door.

CHAPTER 8

Kate heard the elevator car approaching the third floor. Before the shiny steel doors opened, a ding sounded. Kate looked up, her phone pressed against her shoulder and ear as she wrote on her note pad. Connor and Sundae stepped off the elevator.

Sundae ran to Kate's side, nudged her, then sat looking expectantly up at her. Kate quickly closed her drawer so Sundae couldn't get into the cheese treats. Then Kate set down her ballpoint pen and gently massaged Sundae's shoulders. She hung up the phone.

"I missed you at the gym last night," Connor said.

"I took a hot bath, curled up on the couch with

a cup of tea, and read a book. I fell asleep," Kate said, smiling, tilting her head to one side.

"Coming down with something?"

"No, just didn't feel like going."

Connor took off his sport coat and loosened his necktie before sitting at his desk.

"Before you get too busy there, that was Bud Hampton's father I was talking to. He and Mrs. Hampton would like to meet with us to discuss what we're doing on their son's case. Their flight just got in and they wanted to get something to eat at the airport. I told him we'd meet them at Dottie's."

"Did you happen to mention to them that we really don't have anything yet?"

"Just put your coat back on; let's go catch a flight," Kate said, standing.

"I wish I were catching a flight."

"Where would you go?" Kate asked with a smile.

Connor dismissed her question. He didn't want to bring up memories of his broken personal life, marriage, and divorce. Nevertheless, if there was one thing Connor disliked most about his job, it was dealing with the families and friends of the victims. He knew they hurt. They all wanted answers right away, which almost never happened unless you were lucky enough to come across the guy with the smoking gun at the crime scene. It typically took months and sometimes years after he started working a case before he learned the who and the why – and that was if he was lucky. After the trial ended and the judge's gavel dropped for the last time, the result was the same. The victim was still dead and never coming back to their family. The void left by the victim's death would never go away, nor would the pain. Some said that catching the person or persons who caused the harm helped create closure. Yet all too often, families were never the same.

A crime such as the murder of Bud Hampton was like an enormous puzzle with pieces jutting off in this direction and that. In time, a good detective could lay out the entire puzzle with each piece carefully put in its place. However, one piece of the puzzle was always missing. Try as you might to appreciate the work and dedication of this magnificent puzzle on which you worked for month or years, your eye was always drawn to the gaping hole where the missing piece should have been. Nevertheless, it was their job to offer comfort in what they were doing to find the killer.

"What kind of monster would do this type of thing?" Mrs. Hampton asked, dabbing at her deep blue eyes with a tissue. Her face looked tired, as if she had not slept in days and her body was running only on adrenaline. "I simply do not understand who could come into someone's house and kill them in their sleep."

Connor and Kate let Mrs. Hampton vent. They knew this was part of the grieving process, especially when a loved one was lost in such a manner.

"Mr. and Mrs. Hampton, can you think of anyone who would want to harm your son?" Connor asked.

"No one, Detective Maxwell." Mr. Hampton leaned forward, putting both elbows on the table and looking at Connor. His eyes were red.

"Detectives, I know you must hear this a million times in your line of work but Bud was a good man." Mrs. Hampton opened her purse and pulled out photographs of their son. She laid them on the table. One photo showed Bud and Ellie with their arms wrapped around each other. The other was of Bud in a graduation cap and grown. A third photo was of Bud as a teenager in a baseball uniform. Mr.

and Mrs. Hampton looked at the photos for a few moments.

Mr. Hampton cleared his throat, then finished answering the detectives' questions.

"Bud went to the university after high school. When he graduated from the university, he worked at the hospital. As far as we know, he never knew anyone who would do such a heinous thing."

"What did your son do at the hospital?" Kate asked.

"He worked in the IT department."

"Was he in charge of the hiring or firing in that department?"

"No, he was a programmer who worked on proprietary software the hospital used. As far as we know, he never really interfaced with the employees. He answered only to his boss."

"And that was?" Connor asked.

"Oh, what was her name?" Mrs. Hampton looked at her husband.

"Pam. She's the director of the department," Mr. Hampton said.

"Do you have Pam's last name?" Connor asked.

"James. Pam James heads the department that Bud works…I mean used to work in." Mr. Hampton corrected himself as so many families did after the death of a loved one.

Connor jotted down the information. "Do either of you know if Bud and Ellie were having problems?"

Tears rolled down Mrs. Hampton's cheeks. "No, they both seemed very happy." She dabbed at her tears. "We thought they would get married someday."

"Did Bud ever mention any issues with Ellie's ex-husband or any other men in Ellie's life?"

"No, not that I can recall," Mrs. Hampton said.

Connor pulled out a business card, as did Kate. They passed the cards to the Hamptons.

"If you think of anything, please don't hesitate to give us a call," Kate said as she hugged Mrs. Hampton around the shoulders.

CHAPTER 9

The three detectives – Connor, Kate, and Sundae – entered the police department through a door marked "authorized personnel only" in large red block letters. As they neared the dispatcher's desk, they could hear the sounds of radio transmissions. The young dispatcher brushed a lock of auburn hair behind her ear as she looked up from her dispatch log.

"Detectives, a deputy, David Smith, from the Natick County Sheriff's Department wants you to call him ASAP," the dispatcher said as she passed a folded piece of paper to Connor.

"Thanks," Connor said. He, Kate, and Sundae walked back to their desks.

"What is it?" Kate inquired as she unlocked the

old gray metal file cabinet, removed a file folder, and sat at her desk.

"Not sure, just wants us to call."

"Maybe we've been invited to the Sheriff's Department Ball." Kate smiled at Connor.

Connor laughed. "Sheriffs don't have balls."

Kate laughed. "Good one."

Connor dialed the number that was handwritten on the paper. Kate looked over a stack of files. She half-listened to a one-way conversation between Connor and the deputy. Kate quickly looked up when she heard the name Brad Hopper. Connor hung up the phone and stood.

"Let's go."

He and Sundae were already at the elevator door before Kate had time to lock the files in the cabinet.

"Where are we going?"

The elevator arrived, and Connor held the door for Kate and Sundae.

"Highway 10. A couple of kids found some things belonging to Brad Hopper in the brush. When our dispatcher overheard his name, she requested more information from the deputy."

Deputy David Smith showed Connor and Kate a man's red coat along with a keycard that had Brad Hopper's name and photo on it.

"The teenagers found this over there," the deputy said, pointing to a stretch of Highway 10. Sundae sat beside Connor's left leg, her gold shield gleaming in the mid-morning sunshine.

"It was like someone tossed it out of a moving car," Deputy Smith continued. "When I called it in, your dispatcher heard the name I gave on the keycard. We had several deputies do a search for anything else, as she said this was a person of interest in a homicide case you're working."

Connor bent down and held the coat and keycard for Sundae to sniff, then gave her the command to search.

"Work," Connor said.

Sundae ran off, sniffing through the grass and brush in a zigzag pattern. At times, all they could see was the tip of her white tail.

"I can assure you, we did a complete search of this area, Detective."

Connor held the keycard in his gloved hand. He turned it over, looking at it. Kate and Connor looked up when they heard Sundae howling off in the distance. The three walked over and found

Sundae sitting in front of a plastic card lying on its side deep in the tall grass.

"Release," Connor said to Sundae. He reached for the card and turned to Kate. "Gym membership keycard for Brad Hopper."

"I guess we need to pay another visit to Mr. Hopper."

Sundae sniffed around the area until Connor called her back to their unmarked car.

"Mr. Hopper, today a deputy from the Natick County Sheriff's Department found a red coat, a security keycard, and a gym membership card discarded along the side of Highway 10. This in itself would not be an issue, but given the fact that we're investigating a homicide a few miles from where these items were found, I thought we would pay you a visit."

Brad's face flushed as he hesitated for a moment.

"I forgot to lock my car at the grocery store. When I came out, my red coat was missing."

"Did you file a police report?" Kate asked.

"No, I reported at work that the card had been

taken. They deactivated the code on my card and issued me another one."

"I assume we can get a date when they deactivated the card. Surely your company keeps records."

"Yes, of course," Brad said, his voice a little shaky.

"Would you request those records, please?" Kate asked.

Brad picked up the phone and requested the records on his missing keycard.

"A coat that expensive...I assume you reported it stolen to your insurance company," Connor said

"No, I...told you, I just replaced my keycard here at work."

"What about your gym card?" Connor asked.

Brad looked down at his desk. He had never been in trouble with the law in his life. However, he had watched enough TV to know where this type of questioning was going. It appeared to be heading down a very slippery slope.

"No, I was going to but didn't have the time." Brad sounded defensive as he answered their questions. After a few seconds of silence, he said, "I think I should call my attorney."

CHAPTER 10

The elevator chimed as the door opened and Beth Ellis stepped out. Connor looked up, smiled, and strolled over to greet her, with Sundae close behind. Beth gave Connor a big hug, then bent down to pet Sundae.

"I see you still have your faithful partner by your side," Beth said with a smile.

"What can I say? She just can't get enough of me," Connor said, scratching Sundae's ears.

Kate looked the woman over, discreetly sizing her up. Beth wore an expensive midnight blue business suit with matching heels that accentuated her tall, slender figure. A delicate gold pendant and chain hung from around her neck. Not something Kate could ever think of wearing as a detective.

Kate figured that Beth was about her own age, which was thirty. Beth's dark, elegantly styled hair framed her flawless face. Not even a laugh line by her eyes. Kate supposed that Beth was either a Botox queen or belonged to the Wrinkle Cream of the Month club. Was it really possible for someone to have that perfect of a complexion? Maybe she, too, should look into some facial creams. Kate had only a few laugh lines around her eyes. She made a mental note to check out some creams this weekend if she had time. She wondered what brand Beth used.

Connor had told Kate that he had worked with Beth when he was with another police department years ago. Beth had a Ph.D. as a psychologist, but specialized in profiling killers. Connor felt Beth might be able to help them on the Hampton case.

After the exchange of a few niceties, Connor brought Beth over to meet Kate. Upon closer inspection, Kate thought that Beth looked like she belonged on the cover of a fashion magazine. The woman really looked out of place in a stuffy police department, never mind profiling a killer. Two uniformed patrolmen took notice of Beth as they walked to the elevator. They stopped and lingered at the elevator door before pressing the down button.

Kate wondered if any of the guys at the PD admired her that way. After all, thanks to all her Zumba classes, Kate's body was well-toned, with not an ounce of flab. Her auburn hair was its natural color, and she had it cut once a month by a guy named Enrico, who worked downtown. When Kate had attended state college, girls and guys alike had commented on her green eyes.

The sound of Beth's voice brought Kate out of her musings.

"I looked over what you sent me," Beth said, looking at the detectives. "The ME said Bud Hampton was shot at close range, execution-style."

Connor pulled a chair up for Beth to sit on.

"Any large outstanding debts the victim owed, drug or gambling issues?" Beth asked, pulling a yellow legal tablet and pen from her briefcase and crossing her legs.

"No, both the vic and the girlfriend were clean of drugs. So was the house. Bank records showed he worked at the local hospital as a computer programmer. There were direct deposits from the hospital, nothing more. The house and furnishings matched his salary, as did the car he drove. They were living within their means," Connor said.

"Any large withdrawals, maybe to pay off gambling debts?"

"Nothing," Kate said.

Beth sat for a minute, thinking, tapping the end of her pen on the tablet.

"My thoughts are that this is a crime of hate and anger. The crime scene simply doesn't render a home invasion or robbery. May I ask what religion Mr. Hampton was?"

Kate looked through her file. "His funeral will be at the Westside Presbyterian Church."

"That doesn't fit the usual pattern for a hate crime," Beth said, jotting a note on her tablet.

"I go back to anger, then," Kate said, looking at her file and jotting down a few notes.

Connor stood at the white board. "We have several persons of interest." He pointed to Brad Hopper's photo. "He was an ex-boyfriend of the girlfriend. They had lived together for several years, but the girlfriend said the breakup was mutual. His name is Brad Hopper. He has a good job and is engaged to be married this spring. He was out of town at the time of the murder, and he has records to prove it. You know, the usual things … hotel and restaurant receipts."

"Records can lie," Kate said.

"We're still waiting for the hotel camera images to be enhanced. The security personnel didn't see him on any of the images, nor did we see him at first glance. But we need to go over them again. Seems the lobby camera lens wasn't in the best shape."

Beth looked at the board. "I assume you talked to Brad's fiancée to see if they have any issues, any cold feet or longing to go back to his ex-girlfriend?"

"We did. The wedding is set for spring. We also talked with Brad's friends. By the looks of everything, he's clearly moving on with his life. But…"

Connor walked back to his desk, picked up an evidence sheet, and handed it to Beth.

"We were called by a deputy David Smith from the Natick County Sherriff Department. It seems that a few days ago, two teenagers were walking along Highway 10 when they found things that had been discarded by the roadside. The first item was a red coat, men's size large. The second item was a keycard. The third item Sundae found; it was a gym membership card. The IDs all had Brad Hopper's photo and name on them. Added to this equation is the fact that Brad doesn't live in Lakewood. He lives about sixty minutes north of here. However, the items were found three miles from the Hampton crime scene." Connor sat down.

Beth jotted another note on her tablet.

"While the items don't mean Hopper is guilty," Kate said, "when Connor and I returned to talk to Mr. Hopper about what we had found, he lawyered up."

"Did he state that the items were missing?" Beth asked.

"Yes. Before he wanted his attorney, we asked for any documentation about when his office had canceled the code on the lost keycard and when it had issued a new keycard to him."

Beth looked over the board once again, then returned to her notes.

"I keep wondering if there could have been a lovers' triangle," Kate said.

"Anything is possible," Beth said. She quickly changed the subject. "Did you two run an MO crosscheck?"

"We did. Nothing came back as a match within a two-hundred-mile radius," Kate answered.

Beth noted this on her tablet. "Did you get anything back from his attorney as to when the keycard was canceled and a new one issued for Mr.

... ah ..." Beth searched on her tablet and started pulling her file back out of her briefcase.

"Hopper," Kate offered.

Upon hearing this, Beth returned the file to her briefcase.

"From the records his attorney provided, the card from his work was reissued a week before the murder," Connor said, stroking Sundae's long ears.

"Is it possible that the records had been changed?" Beth asked.

"We thought about that, too, Connor replied. "Brad could have changed them or had someone change them for him. It's on a simple paper log – no date or time stamp to validate anything.""Who's the other person of interest?" Beth pointed toward Jeff Gilbert's photo.

Connor answered. "He was Ellie's boyfriend after Brad Hopper and right before she became involved with Bud Hampton. Ellie acted like it was nothing more than casual. In fact, she dropped any communication with the guy after she met Bud. That was over a year ago."

"We requested a search warrant for Brad's house. Maybe we'll glean something from that." Kate held up a piece paper, looking it over.

Beth adjusted her seating as if she was

uncomfortable in such a cheaply constructed chair. The lack of adequate padding in the seat and the chair's wobbly legs probably had something to do with that. Beth tucked the tablet back in her briefcase and stood, straightening her skirt.

"I'll try to work up something for you both by the end of the week." Beth handed Kate her business card. "It was nice meeting you, Kate." Beth shook her hand.

Connor and Sundae walked Beth to the door. The phone rang as Beth stepped into the elevator and the door closed. Connor and Sundae walked back to his desk as Kate hung up the phone.

"That was the DA's office. We have our warrant for Brad's house."

CHAPTER 11

The two CI techs always reminded Kate of a comedy team rather than detectives who specialized in crime investigations. Chris was tall and thin and had a ruggedly handsome look. While he always wore slacks, a dress shirt, and a tie, Kate always thought he would look better wearing a flannel shirt and jeans, like the guy on the paper towels she always bought at the grocery store. Chris had a dry sense of humor. Joe, on the other hand, was a smaller, more muscular man who had what Kate's mom would have called "bedroom eyes." Joe had an odd sense of humor. The two of them could easily have done some moonlighting at the local comedy club.

"So, where's your partner and his four-legged, tail-wagging friend today?" Joe asked.

"They're meeting with the ADA this morning."

"That's okay. We'd rather talk to you. You're much prettier than he is and you don't have four paws like the little sniffer."

Kate blushed and laughed. "What? You aren't smitten by Ms. Sundae?"

Both Chris and Joe laughed.

"We were in the neighborhood and thought you might want to know we 'precinct maids' did the dusting and cleaning on the Hampton crime scene," Joe said. "We didn't find anything out of place on the carpet. Just your standard dust that matched the outside the home, strands of hair that matched the three people living there. However, when Chris vacuumed the rug, we found something you'll want to know about: fibers in the carpet."

"Aren't fibers what carpet is made of?" Kate asked.

"Yes. However, these weren't carpet fibers," Chris said.

"It took us some time to find out what exactly they were, but the fibers are consistent with shoe condoms," Joe said with a smile.

"Shoe condoms?" Kate asked, a puzzled look on her face.

"Joe, be nice to the lady," Chris said. "What Joe's talking about is those covers you put on shoes. You know, so you don't bring dirt into the house. Servicemen wear them on their shoes when they come to work on your cable or something like that."

"We all wear those at a crime scene," Kate said.

"Not this brand, we don't. These are the type you buy at a big-box home improvement store. The fibers are much thinner and are blue, not white like what we wear," Joe said.

"So you think the killer wore shoe covers?"

"Can't say for sure the killer wore them," Chris said. "What I am saying, Kate, is that I found them from the bedroom to the kitchen. I also picked them up in the den by that black backpack that was on the floor."

Kate remembered that this was the path Ellie stated the killer had taken from the bedroom to the kitchen. The backpack was found in the den. It didn't belong to anyone living in the house.

"Whoever this SOB is, he sure put a lot of thought into this before he pulled the trigger that night," Chris said.

Connor and Kate wore white cotton gloves as they searched Brad Hopper's home office. Sundae busied herself by sniffing around. She abruptly stopped in front of the printer stand, then sat and howled, signaling to Connor that she had found something.

"What the…?" Connor looked at Sundae. He gave his release command and lifted the lid on the ink jet printer. When that rendered nothing, he looked around the printer stand.

"Find anything?" asked Kate.

"No, nothing," Connor said. "Guess she's off her game today." Connor looked once more, then walked away. Sundae quickly took her place in front of the printer stand once again, sat, and howled. Connor shook his head and once again gave the command for Sundae to be released. This time, Sundae started pawing at the printer's bottom shelf. In doing so, she knocked over a foot-square fabric storage basket containing typical office paraphernalia. Ballpoint pens, a red plastic ruler, an extra ink cartridge, a box of highlighters, and dry erase markers littered the floor. Connor bent down to pick up the contents Sundae had knocked out of the basket. As he did, he caught something in his line of sight. A pile of papers had been shoved behind the dusty outline of where the basket had once sat. Connor leaned in and pulled out the rumpled stack of papers.

"Is this what you wanted us to see, girl?"

Connor stood and looked over the stack of papers in his hands. Kate approached and stood beside him. Connor stopped, pulled two items from the pile, and studied them. The paper in his left hand was a bright orange flier with a photo of a handgun on its left side. Large block letters advertised a gun show. In his right hand, Connor grasped an admission ticket for the gun show, which had been held months before the murder. Red ink stamped on the ticket indicated that someone had, in fact, attended the show. "For a man who isn't a gun enthusiast, it's funny that he attended a gun show."

Connor transferred each of the items into a separate evidence bag, then took out his pen and wrote down the date, time, and location of its collection. On the line asking for the name of the person had collected the evidence, he wrote his name. Then Connor started putting the pen back into his shirt pocket.

"Don't put that away so quickly." Kate held up a

yellow and white box with a label that said "shoe covers". "The box is supposed to have ten, but two are missing. One for each foot. Maybe these will match the fibers that Joe and Chris found in the carpet," Kate said, handing them to Connor. "Why on earth would Brad Hopper need shoe covers in his line of work? Every time we see him, he's in a suit and tie."

"To kill someone," Connor replied.

CHAPTER 12

*S*everal days later, the lab report came back. The fibers from the carpet did indeed match the eight remaining shoe covers in the box. Connor carefully looked over the report.

Three days after the report on the shoe covers had come in from the lab, Brad Hopper and his attorney sat at one side of the interview table. Kate, Connor, and Sundae sat at the other side. Connor purposely allowed Sundae to enter the interview room. He wanted to see how she would respond to Mr. Hopper. Connor noted that when they had entered the room, Sundae had run to Mr. Hopper's side, sniffed around briefly, then returned to sit down between him and Kate. 'Odd behavior,'

Connor thought, considering Sundae's lack of interest in the suspect.

"Detectives, this better be good. You've disrupted my client's work several times now! No DNA of his was found at the crime scene, plus he has an alibi for the time of the murder," Attorney Ted Kent said sternly, scowling.

Connor and Kate ignored the attorney's theatrics.

"Mr. Hopper, do you use shoe covers for anything at work or home?" Connor asked.

"Shoe what?" Brad looked confused as to what they were.

Kate got up, left the room, and quickly returned with a pair of white shoe covers that she had removed from a package in her desk. She tossed them across the table for Brad to examine.

"Detectives, where are you going with this line of questioning?"

"No, I don't use anything like this at work or home," Brad said.

"Are you saying you never saw a shoe cover before?" Kate asked.

"I've seen service people wear them. Wasn't sure what they were called," Brad responded.

"Can you explain how a box of shoe covers was recovered from your home office?"

"You don't have to answer that," Brad's attorney, Ted Kent, blurted out.

"I have no idea … I never saw them before," Brad said.

"For God's sake, that's it! We're done here, detectives," the attorney said, standing. "Unless you're arresting my client, we'll see ourselves out of here."

Brad stood, his face pale white as he followed his attorney to the door.

"Oh, one last thing," Connor said before opening the door. "Did you or your fiancée happen to attend the gun show last August in Lakewood?" He held up a photocopy of the gun show flier.

Brad turned toward the two detectives. "I…."

His attorney interrupted before Brad could finish.

"No, I'll answer this," Brad said. "I told you, I don't like guns. I purchased one many years ago and sold the stupid thing. I don't like them, nor do I have a need for them. So I would have no desire to attend an event like this." With that, the attorney ushered his client out of the room before Brad could say another word.

Connor looked over at Kate and then at Sundae lying on the floor between them.

"Sundae wasn't the least bit interested in him. Did you notice?"

"I noticed." Kate looked at her watch. "We better get a move on if you still want to go to Hampton's funeral. The Presbyterian church is all the way over on the west side of town.

A closed wooden casket sat on the altar as the minister spoke of Bud Hampton's life and how from the time he was a young boy he had given to and helped others. Connor and Kate stood at the back of the church. While others were there to mourn the loss of Bud Hampton, Connor and Kate were there to observe the actions of the people in attendance. They saw Mr. and Mrs. Hampton in the front row along with Ellie and her daughter, Kim. Two rows back, they thought they saw Kim's father, Sam Peters.

The service lasted just under an hour. Then six pallbearers carried the casket from the church and placed it into a black hearse. At the graveside service, Mrs. Hampton's sobbing could be heard over the minister's voice. After the short service, people shook hands and departed. Connor and Kate were walking back to their car when Mr. Hampton approached them.

"I'll call you tomorrow. It may be nothing, but I remembered something Bud told us."

CHAPTER 13

*C*onnor and Kate immersed themselves in the Hampton case. They pored over the phone records for Ellie and Brad as well as for the victim, Bud Hampton. If Kate's theory of a lover's triangle was correct, there were no calls or text messages to prove it.

"They could have used a burner phone to communicate," Kate suggested.

Connor rubbed his hand through the two-day-old stubble on his face. "Maybe, but…" He stopped mid-sentence as the elevator chimed and three mailroom workers dollied plastic mail tubs toward them.

"What the…?" Kate said.

"Let me guess. The newspapers and TV reports

have brought out all the crazies in the world," Connor said, shaking his head in disgust.

"Where do you want all this?" the mailroom employee asked Kate with a wink and a smile.

Connor pointed to the side of his desk. The tubs were stacked two high in three rows. The empty dollies rattled across the floor as the mailroom employees returned to the elevator.

Connor carefully clipped together the phone records and stuffed them into a file marked "Bud Hampton". The file bore a red "active" sticker on its front. Connor then lifted the first tub of mail and carried it over to an empty five-foot by eight-foot white folding table in the corner of the room. The day-shift employees began crowding around the elevator door, leaving for the day.

"I can stay and do this," Connor offered.

"What, and let you have all the fun reading these crazy notes by yourself?" Kate smiled and tilted her head.

Connor and Kate grabbed white cotton gloves from their desk drawer and then pushed their chairs toward the table.

"How do you want to handle this?" Kate asked.

"Put the crazies in one stack here." Connor pointed to the left side of the table. "And the tips in another, over here." He pointed to the far right side.

They began opening the letters. After they'd gone through the first tub of mail, the stack of crazies far outnumbered the possible tips. Connor lifted the second tub and dumped the letters onto the table. He and Kate continued sorting the letters into piles.

"So, the ADA still doesn't feel we have enough on Brad Hopper to arrest him?" Kate asked.

Connor ripped open another letter and read it. "No. The fact that his coat and IDs were found close to the crime scene isn't enough."

He opened another letter, read it, and added it to the pile marked for the crazies.

"As for the gun show flier and ticket, we're waiting for the show's records as to which guns the vendors had sold. It was a small show, so it didn't have any security cameras. Once we have a list of what was sold, if we find a match, we'll ask for the records."

"Did Mr. Hampton ever call you with what he wanted to talk to us about?" Kate asked.

"No. If we don't hear from him by tomorrow, I'll give him a call. I know it was really hard on both of them yesterday," Connor said. "Hey, you hungry?

It's past six. We could order some food to be delivered."

"What do you want? I'll order it."

"You pick," Connor said as he opened another letter.

Kate removed her white gloves and ordered a large pepperoni pizza with a side of garlic bread for delivery.

Two more tubs of mail and forty minutes later, the elevator chimed. The aroma of freshly baked pizza and garlic bread wafted through the third floor, awakening Sundae. She stood and shook her head, causing the badge that hung from her neck to jingle.

Connor took off his gloves and tossed them onto the table. Removing a pink ceramic bowl from his desk, he measured out a portion of kibble. Connor kept a small bag of dog food in his bottom desk drawer for nights such as this. After he fed Sundae, he refilled her water bowl with fresh water.

"Boy, has she got you wrapped around her paws." Kate laughed.

Kate opened the pizza box, took two paper plates and napkins, and served up two large slices on each plate. She handed one to Connor. Sundae finished her kibble and looked up at Connor with her big brown eyes, begging for some pizza. When that didn't work, Sundae went over to Kate's side.

"You know, I think that reporter, Candy Martin, really likes you. She called and has been asking a lot of questions that don't involve the Hampton case at all," Kate said.

Connor finished a slice of pizza before he answered. "I'm tired of the head games. I'm just not interested in dating or getting involved."

Kate found herself wondering what Connor's ex-wife had been like. They had broken up long before she and Connor had become a team. Kate knew that Connor had worn his wedding ring on a chain around his neck for quite some time afterward. She had seen it once when a perp had been resisting arrest and the chain had dangled loosely outside of Connor's shirt collar. Suddenly, the silence embarrassed her.

"Oh, by the way, did you know she gave the killer a nickname in the newspapers? She calls him the Moonless Killer," Kate said.

Connor shook his head. "I hate when journalists give them names. Just brings out the copycats and fuels the real killer." He wiped pizza sauce from the edge of his mouth. "What about you? You're a beautiful woman. Why is it you're not dating?"

Kate felt her face flush at Connor's compliment. "I guess I don't like the head games, either. He cheated on me. I guess I should have figured that out myself. Suddenly, the intimacy came to a halt. Three months later, I found out it was because he was sleeping with his younger girlfriend. He was being faithful, alright … just not to me, his own wife."

Sundae walked back toward Connor. Suddenly she stopped and howled at one of the last tubs of mail sitting next to his desk. "I know what you're up to, you little beggar. I get up and you'll be on my chair eating my dinner," Connor said as he continued eating his last slice of pizza.

Sundae dug through the tub of mail. Connor stood and dumped it on the floor. Sundae carefully sniffed through all the letters. When she couldn't get to what she wanted, she started digging through the mail on the floor.

"Careful, she'll have a hole through to the second floor," Kate laughed.

When Sundae stopped, she used her paw to pull one envelope away from all the other mail on the floor. Then she howled. Connor and Kate looked at each other. Kate shrugged. Connor retrieved his gloves and opened the letter.

"What's it say?" Kate asked. Walking around her desk, she saw a note comprised of letters cut from a magazine and glued to a plain sheet of paper. Both Connor and Kate read the letter, which said that Brad Hopper had purchased a 9mm from a Lakewood gun show. The letter went on to state the date that the gun had been purchased.

Connor held the letter in his gloved hand and looked at Kate. "Sundae goes crazy over things like this, but if she and Brad Hopper are in the same room, she couldn't care less," Connor said, deep in thought.

"Maybe he isn't her type of guy," Kate joked. She laughed.

"No," Connor said. "I wonder if we're looking at the wrong guy."

CHAPTER 14

*E*veryone knew Mary Lincoln and John Edwards had been dating for six months. What no one knew was that Mary and John had sneaked out that night. Long after his parents had gone to bed, John sent a text to Mary, asking if she was ready. John pulled on his blue jeans and tucked in his shirt. He then removed a box from the top drawer of his bedside table. The screen on his phone lit up with a one-word response from Mary. Yes.

John picked up Mary and pulled his old, black, half-ton pickup truck off a curve on Highway 10. He turned off the headlights, then turned the ignition over to auxiliary with the radio on. The night was perfect. A light swish of almost-transparent clouds perched in the sky, while stars twinkled high above and through the clouds.

For months, John had saved up for the tiny box in his front pocket. He couldn't wait to pop the big question and see Mary's face when she saw the ring. He knew he still had to ask Mary's parents, but this way he would know Mary's answer ahead of time. He would be enlisting in the Air Force in a few months and he just couldn't leave Mary without her answer.

His plan was to ask her to get out of the truck so he could get down on one knee and propose. John reached for the chrome door handle, then stopped as they saw a car slowly pull off the highway. The driver turned off the headlights and slowly crept through the brush before stopping. Through the moonlight, they could clearly see that the vehicle had no emergency lights on top of it, so it wasn't a cop. Who was it?

"Lock the doors," Mary said in a hushed voice.

John hit the door locks and turned off the radio. They sat, almost paralyzed with fear. A man got out of the car and walked to its back. When the trunk light came on, John and Mary watched him unload two large black plastic bags and drag them into the brush. Quickly, the man shut the trunk and got back into his car. Without the aid of headlights, he pulled the car onto the highway. Only then did the headlights come on.

"Did he dump a body?" Mary's voice shook as she spoke.

"I don't know," John said, trying to curb the shaking in his voice. "Should we go see what he dumped?"

"No! We don't want our fingerprints on whatever it is. Besides, we aren't even supposed to be out here. I want to go home, John. Just take me home, now!"

"Shouldn't we at least call the police?" John asked, forgetting about the ring in his pocket.

"John, I want to go home. If you want to call them later, that's up to you. My parents would be so mad if they learned we were out at this hour."

John started the truck and pulled back onto the highway, careful not to take the same path as the car.

"John, don't call the cops. What if this is something and he comes after you or me? Please," Mary pleaded with John.

John pulled his truck to a stop two houses from where Mary lived. They kissed goodnight and she ran to the house.

Once she was inside, John sat there and wondered what he should do about what they had just witnessed. Maybe it was nothing, he reasoned with himself. Lots of people dump things along the highway. But this wasn't along the highway. The guy purposely drove off the highway and into the bushes, then dumped the bags away from the path.

Mary's words replayed in his head. What if the guy came after them if this was, in fact, something illegal they had witnessed? John's father always complained about how criminals were always let back onto the streets. Maybe Mary was right.

CHAPTER 15

*A*t this point in the investigation, the Lakewood Police Department and the County of Natick had chased down more than 2,000 leads and tips. Some had come from local sources, while others from as far away as Canada. One had come from England. The Lakewood Police Department had set up a hotline and hired extra help to filter leads and open mail related to the Hampton case.

One latent fingerprint had been found on Brad Hopper's photo ID card, which had been retrieved from the field along the highway. Investigators had run the print through their local base, which was a database of fingerprints. The local base files were broken down into several sections. One section contained the prints of convicted felons. Another section contained unidentified prints found at crime scenes. The last section contained prints taken for work purposes and included the prints of law enforcement, military, security, or bank employees. When nothing came back on the fingerprint, it was sent for comparison to the state base file, which was much larger. Still, no match was found. The print was then sent to the FBI's database. Once again, nothing was on file. This meant the person to whom the print belonged had never committed a crime, been arrested, or had their prints filed for a work-related reason. Connor knew all too well that an item found in a field could have been handled by someone who had left a print but had nothing to do with the Hampton case.

Ellie had been questioned more than 12 times, and her story never changed. The same went for Sam and Kim Peters. Several others had been questioned as well, including Bud's supervisor Pam James at the hospital, and Jeff Gilberts, an ex-boyfriend of Ellie's.

In her report, Beth Ellis, the psychologist who created the killer's profile, said she felt the killer was very close to either the victim or Ellie Peters. Beth believed the killer was male and that his act of killing had been methodical and well-planned. Further, the fact that the killer had shot the victim at such a close range could only mean that the act was one of deep-rooted anger. Beth felt strongly that at one time the killer had believed he had no control and that somehow the victim did. The killer's actions on the night of the murder were a means of taking back control and redeeming himself.

The ME's report revealed that the victim's system had been clear of prescribed or illegal drugs. Nor did the victim have alcohol in his system.

"I feel like a dog chasing my tail. No offense, Sundae," Connor said.

Kate saw that Connor's frustration was mounting. She herself felt frustrated by the endless leads that turned out to be nothing at all.

"Don't forget, we need to run by the gun store at 10," Kate said.

At 9:15 the phone rang on Connor's desk. "Maxwell," Connor said, answering it.

It was Ellie. Connor put the phone on speaker so Kate could hear the conversation.

"Detective Maxwell, you had asked me if anything was missing the night…Bud was…ah," Ellie couldn't finish her sentence.

"Yes," Connor replied.

"Well, Mr. and Mrs. Hampton and I have been cleaning up the house." Ellie hesitated; the line went silent for a few seconds. "Well…ah…I had a professional photo made of myself for Bud about a month before his…" Her voice stopped again. She simply could not bring herself to say the word "murder". "Anyway, I had a five-by-seven made of it and had it framed for Bud."

"And?" Connor asked.

"The photo always sat in the den on the end table…."

"Yes?"

"It's missing," Ellie said, her voice quivering.

Kate quickly retrieved the crime scene photos from the Hampton file and rifled through them. The photos had been taken only hours after the murder. As was customary, the CIS team member had photographed each room from every angle. Sure enough, the only end table in the den was empty of a framed photo. The table bore only a ceramic lamp and a TV remote. Kate quickly passed the photo to Connor.

"You just now noticed that it was missing?" asked Connor.

"This is the first time I've gone back to the house. I couldn't even…" Ellie hesitated midsentence. "I…was helping the Hamptons clean out Bud's things."

On his tablet, Connor jotted down what Ellie had said. "Anything else missing?" he inquired.

"No, but why would someone take a photo of me?"

"I don't know, Ms. Peters."

Ellie burst into tears. In the background, they could hear her young daughter, Kim, telling her, "Don't cry, Mommy."

"Ellie…Ms. Peters, are you still there?" Connor asked.

"Yes." Ellie's voice was shaky.

"We're working on the case. As soon as we know something…"

Ellie hung up, cutting Connor short.

Kate and Connor sat for a minute, digesting this new information.

"A photo?" Kate looked over at Connor.

"A photo has no value to anyone except the person who wants it," Connor said. "You sure you don't see it, maybe on another table or on the floor?"

Kate carefully looked through the crime scene photos again, then shook her head no. "Did you happen to see her photo in Brad's office or home?" Kate asked.

"I really don't think he'd be stupid enough to have a photo of his ex-girlfriend sitting in plain sight at his home or office with a fiancée around now," Connor said. "However, killers do keep trophies. Maybe he has it hidden away where only he can see it."

"True," Kate said.

Connor stood and locked up his and

Kate's files. "Let's go to the gun store and see if we can finally arrest Brad."

Just then the phone rang.

"Maxwell."

"Detective, this is Mr. Hampton. Do you have a minute?"

Connor sat back down in his desk chair. "Sure. You had mentioned that you or your wife thought of something."

Mr. Hampton cleared his throat. "A few months ago, Bud mentioned that shortly after he began dating Ellie, an ex-boyfriend of hers had started working at the hospital." Mr. Hampton hesitated. "In the same department as Bud."

"Was it Brad Hopper?"

"Hopper? No. His name was Jeff

Gilbert."

Connor motioned for Kate to sit down. "Did your son mention anything else about Jeff?"

"No, just that he worked there and it seemed sort of strange given that Bud and Ellie were now living together. Bud said that Jeff didn't last long. He thought Jeff was fired a few months after he had been hired."

"Did Bud know why Jeff had been fired?"

"No. One day he just didn't show up to work."

Connor drove toward the outskirts of Lakewood. Kate looked out the window as rain dripped down the glass. She listened to the hypnotic rhythm of the windshield wipers. Lakewood had been unseasonably wet that year. The dampness made the temperature feel colder than normal for late January.

"So, what was your first homicide?" Kate asked, turning to look at Connor.

"A guy held up a liquor store… Killed the owner for five dollars in the register and a bottle of whiskey."

"Did you get him?"

"Finally. His cellmate mentioned that this guy was bragging about doing a guy in. Plus, he wanted to cut a deal for less time," Connor said. "When we questioned him, he knew only things the killer could have known. I had refused to release those details to the reporters."

"You still don't," Kate said. "It's not like on TV, where they solve a crime in an hour-long episode, is it?"

"No, not at all. I guess I just wanted to make a difference and help people," Connor said.

"Not to change the subject, but do you think Brad and Jeff could be in this together?"

"I guess anything is possible, like Beth said...but why? That's the question I have to ask myself."

Connor thought about Kate's question as he turned on his signal and exited the highway to State Road 6. When the car slowed, Sundae stood and looked out the rain-soaked windows.

"By the way, did you know the guys back at the PD nicknamed you 'Charlie Brown'?" Kate asked.

"Let me guess. Because I have a beagle, right?" Connor said.

CHAPTER 16

A bell rang as Kate, Connor, and Sundae entered the Ready Aim Gun Store through the heavy, metal, four-panel door. The rustic building was located on the outskirts of Lakewood, just inside the county line. In fact, for years an ongoing debate had questioned whether this particular address was in the City of Lakewood or on County Road 6, making it under the jurisdiction of the county rather than the city.

Kate looked at the moose head mounted on the far wall behind the handgun counter. It was accompanied by an antelope, a deer, a wild turkey, and a brightly colored pheasant. After a few more steps into the gun shop, Sundae abruptly stopped. The fur on her back stood as she emitted a low growl from deep in her throat. She was eyeing an adult stuffed bear on its hind legs, teeth bared, just to her right.

"Release, Sundae," Connor said sternly.

Sundae released but never took her eyes off the bear. Whatever the taxidermist had – or hadn't – done, Sundae still smelled the danger from this beast. She knew it was no cartoon bear like the red one on the Charmin commercials that aired on TV. To Sundae, there was nothing funny about that big black bear. She tucked herself between Connor and Kate, then looked over her shoulder every few seconds to check on the bear's whereabouts.

Neither the gun shop's address nor its standing or mounted dead animals was the reason why the detectives were there that day.

While Connor already knew that no security cameras were on the premises, the store's owner had told Connor that he would gladly obtain records from the gun show and pass them along. However, the police department had not yet received them. The fact was, the investigators had found the gun show flyer and ticket in Brad Hopper's home office. Plus, they had received the letter stating that Brad Hopper had purchased a 9mm Glock at the gun show. Brad Hopper was still a person of interest in the Hampton case.

At first glance, the gun store appeared to be empty at this early hour with the exception of a clerk who stood behind the counter on the far wall.

"May I help you?" asked the man. With his white beard, he resembled a Civil War general.

"Detective Maxwell and my partner, Detective Stroup." Connor showed his shield.

"What can I do for you detectives?" The clerk smiled as he inspected the gold shields and IDs.

"We have reason to believe that on August 12, your store, or one of your vendors, sold a 9mm Glock to a man by the name of Brad Hopper. We believe this gun may have been used in a murder," Connor said.

"August 12," the clerk repeated. "Ah yes, August 12 was during last summer's gun show. Several vendors exhibited their guns that day, so we had a large booth."

"Did you by any chance sell a 9mm Glock to a Mr. Brad Hopper?"

Without a word, the clerk turned and walked into a small office behind the counter. He returned with a record book, which he set on the counter.

With his index finger, he traced down the lines of each registered sale.

"Don't you use a computer for this sort of thing?" Kate asked.

"Sweetie, we use both. I prefer to use the good old-fashioned way, myself. Don't trust those new-fangled things. If it was up to my business partner here, he would use only the computer."

The clerk reached the date of August 12 and stopped. He turned the book around for both detectives to see.

"No Brad Hopper listed for any gun whatsoever. However, we did have several vendors displaying their guns. One of them could have sold the Glock to the gentleman."

Connor felt Sundae pressing into his lower right leg. Looking down, he noticed she had not taken her eyes off the black bear behind them. "Would you have a list of all the vendors, by any chance?" Connor asked.

"We do. In fact, let me make you a copy." The clerk tucked the book under his arm and returned to the office.

Kate looked at Sundae and bent down to her. "Are you worried about that big, bad bear?" She stroked Sundae's long ears, then stood when she heard the sound of the copy machine.

"I looked just in case your theory was right. No gun was sold to Ellie Peters either," Connor said.

"Here we go, detectives," said the clerk as he emerged from the office, then handed them each a copy of the vendor list.

Connor and Kate looked over the list. It contained each vendor's name along with his or her contact information. "Thank you. You've been very helpful," Connor said.

That afternoon, Connor and Kate called on each of the vendors. Some of them were more than happy to help. Others complained, stating that the Second Amendment protected them.

Kate and Connor had to remind these vendors that this was a homicide investigation and if they did not want to cooperate, the police could subpoena all their records. At that point, the vendors were more than happy to produce the requested records for the day of the gun show.

Eventually, the detectives were down to the last vendor. Their hopes had been dashed, as so far no vendors had sold a weapon to Brad Hopper.

Stanley Jenkins, the last person on the list, answered the door on the first ring. He was a short man, about five feet tall, and had a barrel chest. He welcomed Kate and Connor into his house and ushered them to the kitchen table. As he excused himself to retrieve his records, Kate looked around and noticed that an artificial Christmas tree stood in the corner of the living room. She also saw a large deer head mounted on one wall. She was glad Sundae was in the car.

Mr. Jenkins returned quickly with his record book, along with copies of all the receipts for the show. "Brad Hopper, the name sounds familiar. Let me look," he said, setting the record book on the kitchen table. "I did sell a Glock at the show."

He turned the pages and stopped, his index finger coming to rest on a name. Kate and Connor leaned over to get a better look. There it was. On line 23, the name listed next to the make and model of the gun was Bradley Hopper.

"Mr. Jenkins," Connor said as he pulled out a photo of Brad Hopper, "do you recognize this man?"

"Hold on just a minute." Mr. Jenkins left the room and quickly returned with a folder. "Here's the photocopy of the driver's license," he said, laying the copy in front of the detectives. "I even copied the license number of the car he drove." Mr. Jenkins showed Connor and Kate the description and license number.

"Do you have a copy machine here that you could use to make us a copy of both of these?" Connor asked.

"No copy machine, but I can make a copy from my printer, if that's all right," Mr. Jenkins said.

"That would be great."

Connor and Kate remained at the kitchen table while the printer copied the papers.

"The photo on that license just doesn't look right," Kate said.

"I know. I thought the same thing," Connor said.

As they walked to the door, Connor turned back to Mr. Jenkins. "One last thing. Does the name Jeff Gilbert sound familiar, by any chance?"

Jenkins scratched his head in thought. "Can't say that it does."

CHAPTER 17

*C*onnor and Kate drove slowly from Mr. Jenkins' house. As Connor drove, Kate busied herself in the police unit, examining the copy of the driver's license Mr. Jenkins had given them. The rain hadn't let up; rather, the steady rainfall had become a downpour. Visibility was poor, even with the wipers on high.

Kate hardly noticed the weather outside the car and how the branches of the tree-lined state road hung low, soaked with rain. She was too busy comparing Brad's photo to the one on the copy of the driver's license. The copy was grainy at best; therefore, intricate details were hard to make out.

"Connor, the photo on the driver's license just doesn't look like Brad Hopper. Remember when you showed Jenkins the photo of Brad from our file? He said he couldn't be one hundred percent sure. It looks close but…"

"Kate, he also said the man who purchased the Glock was wearing a Western hat with the brim pulled down. That in itself could explain why he wasn't able to definitively identify the man," Connor said. He didn't take his eyes off the wet, winding highway that curved in front of the police unit.

"But he also told us he couldn't be certain the man with the hat was the man in our photo," Kate said. "Look!" She held up the photocopy of the driver's license.

Connor glanced at the photo. As he did, the police unit's tires hydroplaned on the wet asphalt. Connor rapidly corrected his steering before the car began going off the highway, narrowly missing a guardrail.

"Kate, I'll look at it once we get back to the PD."

Kate muttered under her breath, "This photo is not Brad Hopper. The nose is all wrong."

They approached a sharp curve, which Connor successfully navigated. As they came out of the curve, Kate looked up and screamed as Connor hit the brakes. Just ahead, an overturned car lay in their path.

Connor quickly pulled the police unit to the side of the rain-soaked shoulder and engaged the emergency lights on the police unit. "Call it in to dispatch!" Connor yelled as he jumped out of the unit to see if anyone was hurt.

Kate watched Connor run toward the overturned car. Her heart was beating hard and fast, and she felt short of breath for a few seconds. Even Sundae had perched her front paws on the back of the front seat, watching intently. Kate picked up the mic and gave dispatch their location. She reported that they had come upon an overturned car and that they needed a sheriff's officer and an ambulance dispatched to the area.

Connor pulled the driver out and over to the side of the highway and started CPR. "ETA on the ambulance?" Connor asked, glancing at Kate. As she approached, he kept administering CPR.

"They said about five minutes or less. I put the flares behind our car. Anyone else in the vehicle?" Kate asked as she opened the first aid kit. She stacked several 4X4 gauze pads and used gauze wrap to hold the pads in place on the young man's forehead.

"No, it looks like he was the only person. More than likely, by the look of those tires and the lack of tread, he lost control on the wet highway as he came out of that curve."

In the distance, they heard the ambulance approaching the scene. Within a few minutes, two EMTs ran to the victim.

"What do we have?" asked one of the EMTs as he ran to Connor's side.

"Head wound. He was bleeding badly. He had a faint pulse, then stopped breathing. I made sure the airway was clear and started CPR."

"We'll take over from here, detectives."

Connor and Kate slowly walked back to their police unit. Sundae looked at them from the backseat of the car.

"I better let her out to take care of her business. Tell dispatch we'll be heading back to the PD."

Sundae bounded out of the car, sniffing in a zigzag pattern. After relieving herself, she took off into the bushes, sniffing the brush along the way.

Two sheriff's department cars rolled to a stop. Deputy David Smith exited the patrol car, grabbed his rain slicker, and put it on as he walked over to Connor.

"What brings you three out here in the middle of nowhere, Detective Maxwell?"

"Still working on that Hampton homicide." Connor turned, looked back, and pointed at the stretch of highway. "That sharp curve back there can really be a challenge when it's raining."

"Even when it's dry, that piece of Highway 10 can be a challenge," said the deputy.

They heard Sundae howl in the distance.

"Deputy, if you no longer need us, I better find my dog and get us back to the PD." Connor walked off into the thick brush in search of Sundae.

He knew all too well that scent hounds like beagles could be difficult. Sometimes, when left to themselves, they simply wanted to do what came naturally to them as hunters. Sundae was no exception. While she was a well-trained canine, Connor knew she may have simply treed a critter and started howling at it. For the most part, though, she was on point and all work.

"Sundae, come!" Connor yelled in the direction of Sundae's howling.

In a few minutes, Sundae was beside Connor. Her coat was soaked and muddy.

"Look at you," Connor said as the two walked back to the police unit. When he approached the car, he noticed that Kate was still looking over the paperwork Mr. Jenkins had given them. Connor punched the trunk release and grabbed a dry towel to wipe Sundae off.

Kate looked up as Connor got behind the wheel. "Wasn't that Deputy Smith?"

"Yeah. Ms. Sundae must have treed herself a critter back there and was having a blast."

Before Connor could pull back out onto the highway, his cell phone rang. He looked at the caller ID and saw that the call was from Malcolm Greenblatt, ME. Kate half-listened to the call. When Connor hung up, he put on the emergency lights and pulled back onto the highway.

Kate looked over at Connor. "What was that all about?"

"That was the ME. It seems they just had another homicide. He thought it might be the same MO as the Hampton one."

"Is he sure?" Kate asked.

Connor drove as fast as he could back into the city, to the latest crime scene.

"So, we have a serial killer out there?" Kate asked. "Who did they dispatch to the scene?"

"Detectives Bob Barton and Grant Harris."

CHAPTER 18

*B*eth Ellis sat looking at the two white boards. One board had "Hampton" across the top while the other had "Jefferson". On each board, the victim's photo appeared under the name. Beth, Connor, and Kate were meeting with Bob Barton and Grant Harris, the detectives assigned to the homicide of Craig Jefferson.

Bob was a tall man, standing a little over six feet. He was in his late forties and was a seasoned cop, having moved up the ranks from the uniformed division to detective. Grant had been a lateral transfer from a police department out of state. He stood only five-feet-two. Their height differences had led the members of the Lakewood PD to give the detectives their nicknames: "Mutt" and "Jeff".

"We're waiting for all the reports from the ME and the CSI team to come back on this latest victim, Craig Jefferson. I thought this would be a good time for all of us to regroup and compare notes to see if, in fact, we have a match with the two cases," Connor said.

Beth tapped the end of her pen on a yellow tablet. Deep in thought, she stared intently at the two white boards.

Connor continued. "As you may know, Candy Martin's report on the morning show speculated that this is a serial killing."

"Did someone call the TV station with a tip that caused her to come to that conclusion?" asked Bob.

"No. I'm sure this is just for ratings. She asked me for details. I told her that this is an ongoing investigation and that I couldn't comment," Connor said.

"We did the same on the Jefferson case," Grant said.

Beth looked up from the white boards at Connor. "Is there any link to a person or persons in the Hampton case to those in the Jefferson case?" she asked.

"Not so far. But we're still looking into it," Kate interjected.

Beth continued scrutinizing the white boards.

"Both killings occurred early in the morning. Both perpetrators entered the home and killed the victim while they slept in their own bed. Very similar, yes," Kate said. "However, that's as far as it goes at this point."

Connor remained in front of the white boards. "The difference with the Jefferson case is that no one was home except the victim. With the Hampton case, two other people were in the house – the victim's girlfriend and her daughter."

"Very gutsy, if you ask me," said Grant.

"We still haven't ruled out a copycat killer," Bob said, looking at Beth.

"Tell that to Candy Martin." Connor was clearly irritated about the way the media was handling things. He tried to avoid the press. Some of the other officers wanted to be in the limelight. Connor said it was their 15 minutes of fame.

"What's that?" Beth pointed at a sheet of paper taped to the Hampton board.

"That's a copy of the driver's license provided to a gun dealer for the sale of the 9 mm Glock at a gun show to a man named Brad Hopper," Kate said.

Beth glanced back at Brad's photo, then looked through her file. "I thought you said he owned a rifle years ago and didn't have a handgun anymore."

"When we picked up this copy from the gun dealer, Kate kept saying something looked wrong with it. Back here, we compared it to our copy from when we had questioned Mr. Hopper. It wasn't the same license, so we pulled the original DMV record. The photo on file doesn't match what was given to the gun dealer," Connor said.

"We've called Mr. Jenkins, the gun dealer who sold the weapon on the day of the show, and asked him to come in," Kate said.

Connor walked toward the white board, looking it over. Bob and Craig examined the original DMV photo and the copy.

Bob turned around and leaned on the table. "On the Jefferson case, dispatch received a call from Jefferson's sister. When we questioned her at the scene, she said they were planning to have lunch together, like they did every Wednesday. When he didn't show up, she called his cell phone. Our victim didn't answer, so she became worried and went to check on him. She found him dead in his bed. As one of you mentioned, no one was home with him, unlike with the Hampton case. Therefore, we don't have a definitive time when the crime happened.

The ME felt that the victim had been dead at least seven hours before the sister discovered the body."

"There were no signs of struggle, nor was anything out of place," Grant added, looking around the room.

"Not even a photo?" Kate asked.

"A photo?" Bob questioned.

"In the Hampton murder, the girlfriend, Ellie, called several days later to tell us she had noticed a photo that our victim always kept on an end table in the den was missing," Connor explained.

"A trophy for the killer," Bob said.

Beth looked over the crime scene photos and said, "I don't think so, not in this one. I still think the killer in the Hampton case had an intimate connection to the victim or his girlfriend." She walked over to her chair and sat. Crossing her legs, she put her tablet back on her lap and jotted notes.

"Gentlemen, please get back to us once you talk to your victim's sister. If any of the names we have on the Hampton case match, let us know."

Brad Hopper and his attorney sat in the small interview room with a single metal table in front of them. They waited for Connor to enter. Just outside the room, Mr. Jenkins stood in the narrow, darkened hallway, looking at them and listening.

"Mr. Jenkins, is this the man who purchased the Glock from you at the gun show?"

Mr. Jenkins listened to both men talk. As he studied the younger man's face and body language, he shook his head. "No, that's not him."

"Mr. Jenkins, he's wearing a suit and tie now. Could that be throwing you off?" Kate asked softly.

Mr. Jenkins rubbed his hands over his beard and looked once more. "No, that isn't him."

"Mr. Jenkins, this is extremely important. Are you positive?"

Mr. Jenkins moved closer to the one-way glass and looked at Brad Hopper. He shook his head. "I'm one hundred percent sure that isn't the man I sold the gun to."

CHAPTER 19

"You're late," Kate told Connor as he rushed in and hung his sport coat on the back of his chair.

"I had to drop Sundae off at the vet's office to have her teeth cleaned."

Kate smiled at Connor. "Ah…even the K9 gets days off."

Connor looked at Kate and wished, as he had many times, that they weren't partners. He found her extremely beautiful and almost irresistible sometimes. Nonetheless, the policy at the Lakewood Police Department was very clear. An officer was never to become romantically involved with another member of the department whom they worked with. A relationship would be acceptable if Kate worked with someone else inside the department, but with them teamed up, romance wasn't allowed.

"I sure wish Sundae could be here today," Kate said as she walked over and picked up her coffee cup.

"What?" Connor said.

"Where are you today Mr. Maxwell?"

"Sorry, just worried about Sundae, I guess." That wasn't at all what he was thinking about. He felt his face blush.

Kate smiled and chuckled.

"Jeff Gilberts is coming in for questioning today. I thought it would be good to see how Sundae reacted to him. Mr. Jenkins is already in the private lobby, waiting for us."

"That was nice of him to come in again," Connor said. He grabbed his coat and started down the hallway toward the private lobby.

Kate put her hand on his arm and stopped him. "He told me … he feels responsible."

Connor gave her a confused look.

"Why?"

Kate turned Connor around to face her. She looked at him for a second, then responded. "Because he's the one who sold the gun that killed Hampton."

"He's not responsible."

"I just thought you should know."

Connor and Kate entered the private lobby. Mr. Jenkins got up and removed his baseball cap.

"I'm sorry I was a little late this morning. Mr. Jenkins, thank you so much for coming back in. We have another person of interest I'd like you to take a look at today."

"Anything I can do to help."

Mr. Jenkins, Connor, and Kate walked down the hallway. They stopped in front of the same interview room. This time, Jeff Gilbert sat at the table, his arms crossed over his chest. His legs were stretched out under the table. Mr. Jenkins pulled his eyeglasses from his shirt pocket and put them on.

"I can't be sure … I, well, he looks more like the man I sold the gun to than the other man did but…"

Connor nodded at Kate. She took her cue to enter the room and get Jeff to talk. Once inside, Kate asked Jeff a few questions.

"The way he talks … does that help you, Mr. Jenkins?" Connor asked.

"I simply can't be sure. The show was back in August, you know. The one thing I can say for sure is this man seems more like the man I sold the gun to than the man from yesterday."

"Are you sure this isn't the man?" Connor pressed.

"I'm sorry, I just can't be sure."

CHAPTER 20

*J*ohn eased his old pickup truck into the parking lot off Main and 2nd streets. Just beyond the parking lot loomed a large building with an electric blue sign that read "Lakewood Police Department". Next to the sign was a replica of the Lakewood Police Department badge. Mature oak trees and a beautiful manicured lawn surrounded the building. What looked to be a bronze statue of a policeman bending down to talk to a little girl stood a few feet from the front door.

Several police cars were parked close to the building. John drove through the lot, looking for a parking spot. He found the parking places reserved for visitors and pulled his truck into one. As he reached to turn off the ignition, he saw a police car pull into the parking lot close to the building. The officer exited the car, then reached for the handle on the back door. John watched as the prisoner in the backseat kicked the door, striking the policeman in the thighs. The door hit the officer with such force that the policeman fell over. The prisoner bolted from the car, sprinting across the lawn, still in handcuffs. The officer stood and, with a limp, ran after the prisoner.

John quickly shifted his truck into reverse and gunned it toward the other side of the parking lot. Once there, he shifted the truck into park and threw the door open. Jumping out of the truck, he ran after the prisoner and tackled the cuffed man much like he had done with fellow football players in high school.

"Thank you…?" the officer said, out of breath as he approached.

"John. John Edwards, sir."

"Where did you come from?"

"I had just pulled in." John motioned to the other side of the police department building. "I was about to go in when I saw him knock you over and take off across the lawn." John stood and brushed the grass off his blue jeans.

"Ever think about joining the police force?"

"No, sir," John answered as he watched the officer lift the prisoner to his feet.

"You're a natural, kid. Most people would have been afraid to get involved." Reaching into his shirt pocket, the officer handed John his card. "Call me sometime. I'll buy you a coffee and we can talk some more."

John got back into his truck. Mary's words replayed in his mind as he pulled out onto 2nd Street and left the police department. He wanted to report what they had seen several nights ago and had every intention of doing so. That was until the prisoner almost got away. He thought more about what his dad said about prisoners. They always seemed to get out of jail, one way or another. Maybe he needed more time to think this over.

That evening, John reached into his pocket and found the business card. On it were Officer Randy Simon's name and a phone number. John pulled out his cell phone and dialed the number.

"Lakewood Police Department, may I help you?"

John hesitated for a second. "Ah … I'd like to speak to Officer Randy … Simon, please?"

"Is this an emergency?"

"No, I just wanted to speak to him."

"Your name and a number where he can reach you?"

John quickly gave the woman his name and cell phone number. Randy called back. Under the pretense of being interested in becoming a police officer, John met him at a chain coffee house. Randy gave John the rundown of joining the Lakewood Police Department. As they were about to leave, John sat back down.

"Officer Simon, my wanting to talk to you ... this wasn't about becoming a police officer."

Officer Simon sat back down with a confused look on his face.

"I wasn't at the police department today to pay a parking ticket like I told you," John said.

Officer Simon studied John's face.

"I was…" John looked away, then back at Officer Simon. "The other night, my girlfriend and I snuck out of our houses after hours."

"John, that's hardly a crime. That's more your parents' issue to deal with."

"I know. It isn't the fact that we snuck out of the house. We were parked out along Highway 10. I had bought a ring and was going to ask her to marry me."

"Okay." Officer Simon waited, wondering what

on earth was eating this young man who had come to his aid that morning. He seemed like a good kid.

"We were parked there for maybe a few minutes when a car pulled off the side of the highway." John took a sip of his latte. "The person turned off his lights, got out of his car, and pulled two large bags out of the trunk."

"You said 'his.' Do you know for sure this was a male?"

"When the trunk light came on, the figure looked like a male."

"Did you or your girlfriend recognize him?"

"No, not at all. Mary ... she's my girlfriend ... was really scared and wanted to go home as soon as he left."

Officer Simon pulled a small pad of paper from his chest pocket and wrote down everything John told him.

"Did the guy leave right away?"

"Yes. As soon as he dragged the second bag into the brush, he pulled back out with his lights off until he was back on the highway."

"Do you know what he dumped?"

"No. Mary wanted to leave right away. I never even had the chance to ask her to marry me."

"Could you take me to the place where you were parked?"

"Sure. I think I can find it again."

"Let's go."

onnor and Kate, along with Sundae, walked down the hallway toward the back door. A city maintenance worker swabbed the floor with his mop. He never looked up at the three of them. The old round clock on the wall read 4:15.

"Can I expect to see you at the gym tonight?" Kate smiled at Connor.

Sundae trotted ahead to pay her routine visit to the police dispatcher before she and Connor left for the night. The back-and-forth chatter of radio transmissions between officers of the Lakewood Police Department echoed throughout the hallway.

"Well, hello there, Ms. Sundae! Are you getting ready to go home for the day?" The dispatcher, Sandy Curtis, rubbed Sundae's soft, long ears.

Sundae sniffed around Sandy's desk, looking for treats.

Sandy Curtis was a pleasant, heavyset woman with curly gray hair and silver-rimmed glasses. She was considered the department "grandmother" because she often baked cookies and other treats for her co-workers. She had an especially soft spot for Sundae.

"I know what you're looking for."

Sandy reached into the overstuffed bottom drawer of her desk, making a personal note to someday clean out that drawer. Once she felt the treat bag, she pulled it out. Sundae sat and looked up expectantly.

"Don't you tell your daddy about this. He has this crazy notion that you're not to accept treats from me," Sandy said as she pulled out a treat. Petting Sundae with one hand, she held out the treat with the other. "Just plain rubbish, I say. I bet you feel the same way."

Connor and Kate walked up to the dispatch desk.

"Are you bribing an officer of the Lakewood Police Department?" Connor asked as Sundae swallowed her treat.

Sandy put the green bag of dog treats back in

her drawer. "Would I do that?" The dispatcher gave Connor an innocent look.

"You're going to ruin her for duty, you know that?" Connor smiled. "Not to mention her figure."

Sundae ran to Connor's side.

"You three have a good night."

Kate looked over her shoulder at the dispatcher. Sandy winked as she hit the buzzer under her desk, allowing them to open the door to the parking lot. She watched as the steel door closed and locked behind Connor, Kate, and Sundae.

"27 PD, I'll be 10-6 with a male passenger, John Edwards. We'll be checking out a suspicious dumping he witnessed on Highway 10. If there's anything out there, I'll need you to dispatch county," Randy said.

"10-4," replied the dispatcher. She opened her desk drawer to clean it up. Then, shaking her head, she closed it.

Randy replaced the mic and turned to John. "Okay. Whereabouts on Highway 10?"

"Do you know the curve all the kids call 'Dead Man's Curve'?"

Randy smiled at John and focused his attention on the traffic. "That curve has been called that for years. If memory serves me right, I think it was around 1950 that it got its name," he said.

Within 15 minutes, John was pointing to a path of tire tracks cutting through the dried grass that disappeared into the brush. Officer Simon pulled his car off the highway and called in his location to dispatch. He and John got out.

"We were up there, beyond the little bluff, that night." John pointed. "The car pulled off maybe a little farther than you did. Then he got out. He pulled each bag out one at a time and carried them off in that direction." John turned and pointed toward a densely covered area of brush, due south of the bluff on which he and Mary had parked that night.

Randy and John walked in the direction John had indicated. They were careful to not disturb any tracks. Before long, the two men were in a section of brush so tall that it rose over their heads. The brush was so thick, they had trouble going any farther.

Randy stopped and radioed dispatch. "27 PD, are Detective Maxwell and his canine still on duty?"

"No, but they're on call. Do you need me to dispatch them to the area?"

"It may be nothing, but I think Maxwell's dog would be able to find anything in this thick brush better than a human could. County doesn't have a canine, so ask Detective Maxwell if he would mind bringing her out here."

Officer Simon turned to John. "You're sure this is where you saw him go?"

"Yes, sir."

"I guess animals could have dragged the bags off. Did they look heavy, like the guy was straining to carry them?" Randy asked.

"He was tall, about six feet, and had a medium build. I remember he had one hand at the top and the other supporting the bottom. That's all I can tell you," John said, looking around.

Several minutes later, Connor and Sundae pulled up alongside Officer Simon's car. Officer Simon brought Connor up to date on why they were out there. Meanwhile, Sundae ran in a zigzag pattern, sniffing the ground. She ran into the thick brush. For a moment, only the white tip of her tail was visible. Then that, too, was out of sight.

"You know this is really the county's jurisdiction, right?" Connor said.

"The tip came into me. I'm simply following up on the tip," Randy said.

As the evening sky faded, Sundae began to bay.

The three men walked in her direction just as Kate's unmarked unit rolled to a stop.

"I heard the call. What do we have?" she called out.

"This young man witnessed someone dumping two large bags out here several nights ago."

Kate looked over the terrain. "Wasn't this where we helped county with that wreck the other day? When Sundae ran off into the bushes baying and you thought…"

At that, Connor led the four into the brush, where Sundae sat in front of a large thirty-nine-gallon trash bag.

"Release," Connor said to Sundae as she continued searching the area.

Connor and Kate each fished a pair of gloves out of their pockets. Then they bent down and untied the bag.

The first item Connor retrieved was a loaded clip from a Glock 9mm. Next was the ID containing Brad Hopper's name and another person's photo.

"This must've been the one the guy gave to Mr. Jenkins, the gun dealer."

"Are you thinking what I'm thinking?" Kate asked as she looked at Connor.

Connor pulled a black ski mask out of the bag.

Kate took out a penlight and studied the ID.

"This photo is much clearer than the copies we saw. This really looks like Jeff Gilbert."

"Maybe the two were working together?"

"Or maybe Jeff and Ellie were working together," Kate said.

"Call dispatch and have them get our CIS team out here. I'll need a complete statement from John as to time, date, what he saw, any description of the car and the person he saw," Connor said to Simon.

"Do you want county dispatched?"

"No. I think this may be linked to the Hampton homicide we're working."

John swallowed hard; the word "homicide" played over and over in his head. For a second, he felt dizzy, like his legs would give out on him. Mary had told him not to get involved, as she feared that the person would come after them.

John's thoughts were silenced when Sundae began baying again.

Connor pulled several branches back, allowing Kate and him to walk about ten feet beyond where the first bag lay. They found another black thirty-nine-gallon bag. This one was torn open. Kate could clearly see two shoe covers, like those found at Brad's house. She also saw a cowboy hat.

CHAPTER 22

*B*eth stood, staring silently at the objects on the large table in front of her. Each object had been used in the act of murder. Her mind pictured how each object had been used to either prepare for the crime or to actually commit it. She couldn't explain why her mind worked differently from the minds of the other profilers she'd worked with in the past. She didn't know how she was able to picture objects being used. Sometimes this ability was a gift. Other times it was a curse – one that haunted her when she and the law enforcement agencies couldn't catch the perp and put the scum behind bars.

She wore latex gloves, as did Connor and Kate.

"CSI is checking everything for prints and DNA," Kate said.

"There won't be any," Beth said without even a glance in Kate's direction.

Kate looked over at Connor and mouthed the words, "How would she know that?" She shrugged.

The table held the contents of the two black trash bags that had been recovered. Connor and Kate, as well as the CSI team, had already examined and cataloged each item. They had called in Mr. Jenkins, the gun dealer, who had sold the Glock 9mm on the day of the gun show. Mr. Jenkins had arrived earlier that morning and said that the cowboy hat was just like the one worn by the man who had purchased the Glock 9mm. He indicated that the extra ammo clips looked to be the same ones he had included with the gun sale. The ammunition also matched the ammo used in the Hampton case.

Kate called in the department sketch artist and asked him to create a composite sketch of Jeff Gilberts wearing the cowboy hat they'd found. Mr. Jenkins said that the man who had purchased the gun had worn the hat with its brim pulled slightly down, covering a portion of his face. Upon seeing the sketch, the gun dealer positively identified Jeff Gilberts – not Brad Hopper – as the man to whom he'd sold the gun. Connor and Kate wanted to make sure they'd dotted every I and crossed every T before going to the DA.

Detectives Bob Barton and Grant Harris had come by earlier. Other than the fact that the handgun was the same caliber, nothing matched their Jefferson case, including the extra ammo.

Beth reached across the table and picked up the black ski mask. "Expensive brand," she said. "Most perps would buy something cheap, knowing they'd be discarding it after they'd used it."

Beth asked for the file that Connor held in his hand. She thumbed through it, then stopped at Jeff Gilbert's photo. She looked back at the ski mask.

"Refresh my memory. When did Gilbert and the girlfriend break up?"

"Almost a year ago, but the odd thing is, they went out only a couple of times," Kate said.

"Define 'a couple of times'. Were they intimate? Did they live together?"

"No, they didn't live with one another. She told us they were very casual. Actually, she and Brad broke it off. She dated Jeff Gilbert a few times, then moved on. But she and Brad lived together at that time; they just weren't a couple any longer. They dated other people."

"Brad was okay with that? Did you search Jeff Gilbert's home?"

"No. We focused on Brad first," Kate said. "We wondered whether Jeff and Brad, or even Ellie, could have been in on this together."

"Any life insurance?"

"Yes, but the policy was never changed from Hampton's mother to the girlfriend," Connor said. "Nor was the girlfriend aware of any life insurance. Anyway that's what she said." Connor stood next to Kate, watching Beth.

"He manipulated both of you. This was his plan from the beginning," Beth said.

"What…" Kate had enough of Beth and started to cut her off. Connor reached for her shoulder to stop her.

Beth sat down and looked at Connor and Kate.

"The killer wants anyone and everyone in Ellie's life out of the way. This way, in his deranged mind, she will come back to him and only him," Beth said.

She stood back up and turned to the table as if in a trance.

"He's a person of privilege. He isn't used to hearing the words 'no' or 'wait.' Does that fit Jeff Gilbert's profile?" Beth asked.

"I asked him to come in for questioning. He's coming in tomorrow, if you'd like to listen in."

"I'll pass. I have to be in court. If you don't need me anymore, I'll be going. I have to prepare for tomorrow," Beth said.

Connor turned back to his desk and quickly glanced at the Hampton file.

"Do you buy into the business that after a few dates, this guy could want everyone out of this woman's life? Why didn't he kill Brad…unless the two were in on it together," Connor said. He dialed a number on the phone. As it started ringing, he put the phone on speaker. Connor held up his hand to Kate, indicating that she shouldn't answer his question.

The ringing stopped when they heard Jeff Gilbert's voice in the form of a message. Connor left his name and call-back number, then disconnected.

"You were about to say?" Connor asked Kate.

"If Jeff killed Bud Hampton and framed Brad, the two of them would be out of the picture," Kate said.

"True." Connor sat and thought for a second. He nodded. "Let's grab some lunch."

Kate smiled at Connor. She stood and grabbed both of their files, locking them in the filing cabinet.

"So, what's it going to be today? Italian or Mexican? My treat," Connor said.

CHAPTER 23

The gym was crowded. Kate practiced her kickboxing while she watched the front door out of the corner of her eye, looking for Connor. Just after 6 p.m., Connor pulled the gym door open. Kate smiled. The man looked sexy, even in old sweats and a t-shirt. No matter what he did with his hair, an unruly dark lock curled on his forehead.

Connor waved at her, and then walked over to the free weights. Kate watched Connor as he stretched out his muscular arms, then moved on to stretching his legs. She noticed a few other women in the gym eyeing him. Kate felt a streak of jealousy, then guilt. She knew that, due to departmental policy, she and Connor could never date. She could put in for a transfer within the department, but at the time the only position she was aware of was in auto theft.

She sighed heavily. Why on earth did life have so many difficulties? Even if she did transfer, the possibility existed that he wouldn't be interested in dating her.

Connor interrupted her thoughts. "Hey, how about we grab a bite to eat after we're done?"

Kate pulled out her ear buds, draped them over her shoulders, and smiled at him. "What?" She'd heard him, but she wanted to hear his voice again.

"After we get done here and shower, why don't we grab a bite to eat?"

"Actually, I have my world-famous spaghetti sauce simmering on the stove. Why don't you grab Sundae and come over to the house when you're done?"

"A home-cooked meal!" Connor said enthusiastically. "I'll never pass that up. What can I bring?"

"Surprise me," Kate said, tilting her head to one side.

Kate showered, slipped on a pair of faded jeans and a V-neck sweater, and dabbed a little perfume behind each ear and on her wrists. Hurrying, she went into the den and loaded the CD player with soft background music. Then she quickly set the table for two. She lit candles and stood back, looking at the table.

"No," she said out loud. Shaking her head, she quickly snuffed out the candles, thinking they were too much. Off to the kitchen she ran. She pulled out the bowls that she kept on hand for when Sundae came to visit. She looked at the corner of the living room to make sure Sundae's bed still had a small blanket.

"Where did I put Sundae's blanket?" she thought out loud. Then she remembered; she had washed it the last time Connor had let Sundae spend the weekend with her while he went mountain hiking with a buddy of his. Quickly, Kate retrieved the small pink blanket from the linen closet and placed it to one side of Sundae's bed. Standing back, she looked at the tiny handmade toy box next to Sundae's bed.

Back in the kitchen, Kate ran some water into a large pot. Once Connor and Sundae arrived, she would start the pasta. She began cutting up fresh vegetables and tossing them into a salad bowl. Just as she finished, the doorbell rang.

Before opening the door, Kate glanced at her

image in the foyer mirror and ran her hands through her hair. Sundae immediately ran into the kitchen, following the aroma of spaghetti sauce and the garlic bread cooking in the oven.

"Well, just make yourself at home, Sundae," Connor said, smiling at Kate.

Kate laughed as she watched Sundae sniff around the kitchen.

"You sure this isn't too much work?" asked Connor.

"The sauce was already made. I would only eat my portion and put the rest in the freezer for other meals. In fact, I'll give you some to take home for your freezer," Kate said with a smile. She gave him a friendly hug and shut the front door.

Connor handed Kate a bottle of White Merlot. "It's already chilled," he said.

Connor inhaled the soft fragrance of Kate's perfume. He watched her go into the kitchen and start the pot of water to boil. He missed having a family, missed the smells of home cooking and the touch of a woman.

"What can I do?" he asked.

"Relax. Sundae and I have this. Just sit down."

Connor walked around Kate's living room, looking at photos of Kate and her parents, and another of Kate and her younger sister. He came across Sundae's toy box and bent down to look at it. Connor saw Sundae's name on the front of it and smiled.

"Looks like Sundae has a home away from home here."

After dinner, they each sat down with a glass of wine. Sundae curled up in her bed and quickly fell asleep.

"Dinner was wonderful, Kate."

"We should do this more often." Kate smiled and turned to Connor.

He reached out and placed a hand softly on her face, looking into her eyes. They leaned in and kissed passionately. His kiss was intoxicating. Kate felt lightheaded. Though lost in the moment, Kate pulled back suddenly.

"Connor, if we continue this, you know we can't work together anymore."

Connor quickly stood. "I'm sorry, I shouldn't have…"

Kate wasn't sorry. She'd wanted a relationship with Connor for some time. She stood and wrapped her arms around his muscular shoulders, then leaned in to kiss him again. This time, Kate didn't care about departmental rules, their chief, or their sergeant. She cared only about the man who stood before her.

Suddenly, Connor's cell phone rang. He pulled away to answer it. Kate sat on the couch and waited until Connor disconnected the call.

"That was the IT department. They checked all of Ellie's social media accounts. Seems as though Jeff has been stalking her online for some time," Connor said. He returned his phone to his pocket and took Kate's hand. "Kate, when we're both thinking straight, I think we need to think about where this could lead us."

Kate knew all too well that Connor wasn't talking about the case. The question was, did they really want to end their professional relationship and pursue an intimate relationship with each other?

"You're right," Kate said reluctantly. She went into the kitchen and put some sauce into a few containers for Connor to take home. "Just pop them into the freezer. Take it out in the morning when you want to eat it, and leave it in the fridge. Warm it up in a pan while you boil some pasta." She reached over and gave him a friendly peck on the cheek.

After Connor and Sundae left, Kate cleaned up the kitchen. Suddenly, she heard a text from Connor come in on her phone. It read simply, "I'm sorry."

Under her breath, she said, "I'm not."

When the kitchen was clean, Kate poured herself half a glass of wine. She lit the candles and turned out the lights. Listening to the soft music, she thought about Connor. What was the difference, she wondered, between being a couple and working with that person as your partner on a daily basis, being in love with that person and not being able to show those feelings? Would a person react differently in a situation on the streets?

CHAPTER 24

Connor came in early the following morning. They had a meeting with Jeff Gilbert scheduled for 8:00 and he wanted to write out his list of questions to ask. Looking up at the wall clock, he thought, 'Kate must be running late.' He wondered if they could get past what had happened the previous night. He also wondered whether, if not for their work, things would have progressed further that night. He knew he wanted them to. He remembered the taste of her lips and how soft they'd felt against his. Her body felt much different in an embrace than it did when they were wrestling a perp in the streets. It had felt right to be there with her and Sundae the previous night. It all felt so perfect. Her house had smelled good when he entered, and it had a feminine touch, with each thing in its place. It was not at all like his place, with its bare walls and shelves. He missed having a woman in his life. Was Kate that woman?

The elevator chimed, interrupting his thoughts. Kate rushed in.

"Forget to turn on your alarm?" Connor joked as Kate rushed to her desk and locked up her purse. "We have Jeff Gilbert coming in at 8:00."

"No, we don't," Kate said, looking across her desk.

"I've been here since 6 and no one told me that."

"I was coming in when dispatch received a call from his attorney. It seems Mr. Gilbert has lawyered up. Our schedule and the attorney's don't match. They want to know if they can meet with us tomorrow afternoon."

Connor leaned back in his chair, shaking his head. "I did a little research on Jeff. Seems he comes from a very wealthy family. Dad's a homebuilder and Mom's a psychiatrist."

"That would explain the attorney."

"What explains the attorney?" Connor looked confused.

"Jeff hired Slater."

Connor's eyebrows rose and he leaned forward. "You mean Bennett Slater…the best and highest paid defense attorney the state has to offer? And every DAs worst nightmare."

"The same," Kate said.

Sundae got up and went to Kate's desk. As Kate rubbed Sundae's soft ears, she wondered how the dog had felt about her and Connor the previous night. Sundae had seemed to be comfortable with the two of them together at the house. Then again, Sundae spent almost every day with Connor and Kate.

"Kate…earth to Kate."

"Oh. I was just wondering if Jeff's mommy will go for an insanity plea if Jeff is found guilty, with her being a psychiatrist and all." That was only partly true, but Kate didn't want to bring up the previous night or what she was really thinking unless Connor did so first.

"I requested the subpoena for Jeff's cell phone records from the ADA. Ellie's social media records came in, so we need to go over them when we can," Connor said.

"Give 'em here," Kate said, holding out her hand. "I'll do that."

"They're all electronic. I can send them to your

computer." Connor quickly forwarded the files. "Beth sent us a text early this morning." He read from his cell phone. "She said we should stop looking at the murder and the crime scene for answers. We need to focus on the power behind the act, what drove this person to commit murder."

Kate began looking at what Ellie had posted. First, she found several photos of Ellie and Bud from a weekend getaway. She also found playful photos of the two of them. Next, Kate looked through the account activities, which could be obtained only from the social media site. There, she saw Jeff Gilbert's name and the IP address of the computer used to access and view her account. Below this was a list of time and date stamps for all the instances in which someone had viewed Ellie's page. She scrolled down. 'There must be hundreds,' she thought.

"Come here," Kate said, pointing at her computer screen. "Jeff was cyber stalking her for months after they broke up."

Connor came up behind Kate and looked over her shoulder at the computer screen. "Looks like Ellie thought they were just a few casual dates, but Jeff was on an entirely different page. Maybe this was the power Beth was talking about. The man simply thought more of their relationship than Ellie did," Connor said.

"I'll go down to our IT guys and ask them to take a look at these files, see if the IP address goes back to Gilbert," Kate said. She got up from her desk and left.

Connor picked up his desk phone and pressed the speed dial for the DA's office.

Over the next few weeks, Attorney Bennett Slater's office had called and canceled multiple times. Connor knew all too well that this was a stall tactic to buy them time. Connor had a detail watching Jeff to make sure he didn't leave.

Detectives Bob Barton and Grant Harris had made an arrest in their case. This had taken the heat off the department in terms of the news media and the revelation that this was not a serial murder.

Connor had a meeting downtown with the DA's office about the Hampton case. Meanwhile, Kate stayed behind, working on the paperwork that the DA needed. Her desk phone rang.

"Detective Stroup."

"Detective, this is the office of Bennett Slater.

He needs you to meet him at Highway 10, where the alleged bags were found. We've discovered some very vital objects."

Kate quickly locked up her files and headed for Highway 10.

Minutes later, when they returned to the police department, Connor and Sundae greeted the dispatcher.

"I thought you and Sundae would be out at Highway 10," the dispatcher said.

"Why would we be there?" asked Connor.

"Kate was meeting Bennett Slater there," she answered.

"Slater…See if you can reach her by radio!" Connor said.

"She's not answering," the dispatcher said.

"I can hear that. Try her phone." Connor turned around and ran for the door. Sundae followed him. "If you reach her, tell her I'm on my way. Also, have the IT guys check the phone logs. I want to know the number that called Kate," Connor shouted as the door closed.

CHAPTER 25

Connor weaved in and out of traffic with lights flashing and siren shrieking.

"Get out of the way!" Connor screamed at the motorist who ignored the unmarked car with lights and siren behind her. The woman driving in front of him refused to move her car over so that Connor could pass her on the two-lane highway.

"Give me a break, lady!" Connor said to himself as he pounded his steering wheel. As soon as the oncoming traffic lane cleared, Connor pulled into the lane, passing the woman. "If someone in her family needed emergency help, you can bet she'd want them to pull over," he said to Sundae.

Just as Connor crested the hill, he saw a logging truck in his lane.

"Oh, for the love of…." Connor didn't have to finish the sentence, as the trucker pulled his large rig to the side of the road, allowing Connor to pass.

The voice of Sandy Curtis, the dispatcher, came over the police radio. "15, I have the information you requested."

"15, go ahead PD," Connor said.

Sandy heard the stress in his voice. "I called Slater's law office. They stated no one called here."

"10-4. What about the phone number? Has that come back to anyone?"

"I have the IT people working on that. I'll give you that when it comes in."

"15 PD, put a BOLO out on Kate. Do you remember what she was wearing? If so, give that information and the time she left the PD."

"10-4, 15. Will do."

Sandy had already started preparing a BOLO – an acronym for "be on the lookout" – in case it was needed.

"Also, PD, see if Detectives Barton and Harris can run by Jeff Gilbert's home. If he's there, I want him and his mouthpiece attorney brought in for questioning. Also, I want a make and model of his car and anywhere he might be."

"10-4. Oh, Connor, we'll find her," the dispatcher said without using code.

About eight minutes before getting to the grassy path, Connor turned off the lights and siren. If Jeff Gilbert had lured Kate to this desolate area, Connor didn't want to announce his arrival with sirens blaring and light flashing. However, if his own heartbeat could be measured in decibels, Jeff would know that Connor was coming after him, as Connor's heart was pounding out of his chest.

Connor parked about an eighth of a mile from the grassy pathway and got out of the car. He commanded Sundae to stay by his side as they walked down the old highway. Once at the path, he saw Kate's police unit in the brush. Fresh tracks from the side of her car led in and back out to the highway. Connor put Sundae in search mode and she began her zigzag hunt for Kate. He watched as the tip of Sundae's white tail disappeared into the thick brush until she was completely out of sight in the taller, denser brush.

Looking in Kate's police unit, Connor swallowed hard when he saw that the cord to her police radio had been cut. He used the spare key – they each had one to the other's police unit – to pop the trunk. It contained flares, a first aid kit, a drug kit, and other police paraphernalia. Connor shut the trunk, then looked around for anything. Only an occasional car on the highway broke the silence.

He began searching the area. A breeze had arisen and caused the branches of the bushes to knock together. The sound reminded Connor of his days in a homicide investigation class. The agent conducting the class had carried in a skeleton. The branches sounded like the bones of a skeleton knocking together. The thought made the hair on the back of his neck stand on end.

It was then that he heard Sundae howling off in the distance, signaling to him that she had found something. Connor ran toward Sundae. The thick brush snapped and crackled under his feet. He grabbed his arm as a branch cut through his shirt. Had he stopped long enough to grab his sport coat, he thought to himself, he would have given his arms some protection. Looking down, he noticed a tear and blood on his right thigh as well. When he turned, a branch snapped against his face. Droplets of blood rolled down his cheek.

Five more yards and he found Sundae sitting in front of a woman's scarf. It was Kate's. Connor knew it because she always wore it around her neck with her winter coat.

"Release," Connor commanded. Sundae got up and continued searching the area. Connor grabbed a pair of latex gloves from his pocket. The scarf had blood on it. Was it from the branches, as he had just experienced? Or was it worse? Why hadn't Kate waited for him to get back from the DA's office so they could both go?

Sundae returned to Connor, which meant she hadn't found anything else.

Connor and Sundae ran back to their police unit.

"15, PD, I located Detective Stroup's unit. The mic cord to the radio has been cut. We found only her scarf with blood on it. Anything from Barton and Harris?"

"They're at Gilbert's home right now."

"10-4," Connor said as he swung the police unit back out onto the highway.

CHAPTER 26

*J*eff Gilbert had been unable to keep a job his entire adult life. He still lived with his parents in a sprawling estate 45 minutes from Lakewood. The grounds were meticulously manicured, even at this time of year. Word was the place was worth some 6.5 million dollars. Regardless of the price tag, it was clear to anyone who drove down the driveway that the home was a place of wealth and prestige. To the right side of the large home was a six-car garage with the garage doors pulled down. The only thing out of place was the unmarked police car in the circle driveway under the large portico in front of the home. Detectives Barton and Harris emerged from the front door. They quickly got into their unit and pulled down the long, tree-lined driveway. A woman's face could be seen peering from the front window of the Gilbert home.

"89, PD, Detective Barton and I will be en route to the Gilbert construction site on West and 14th. Please advise Detective Maxwell that Jeff Gilbert was not at home. His mother told us he has been working with his father and would be there on site.

"10-4, 89. Did you copy that, 15?" Sandy wanted to make sure Connor had heard where Barton and Harris were heading.

"Copy that," Connor said. Pulling over his car, he dialed Beth's cell phone, which went straight to voice mail. He thought that was odd, knowing this was Beth's day off.

As he hung up and reached to put the car back into drive, the phone rang again. The caller ID said it was reporter Candy Martin.

"Connor, this is…"

"I know who it is," Connor said.

"Well, hello to you, too. Someone piss in your Wheaties this morning?"

Connor was in no mood to talk to Candy, or to any reporter for that matter. "Listen, I'm busy right now," Connor gruffly said and started to disconnect the call.

"Wait, Connor, we have Kate's photo running as a missing person. I'm only trying to help."

"Thanks," Connor said.

"Please keep us updated and let us know if there's anything we at the station can do," said Candy.

"Will do."

It had been two days since Kate had gone missing. The DA finally came on board, setting aside the fact that Jeff Gilbert came from a wealthy, prominent family with the highest priced attorney in the state.

Connor sat in the squad room, watching the tiny TV screen as Candy Martin reported live from the Gilbert home. Mrs. Gilbert pleaded to the camera for Jeff to do the right thing: to turn himself in and not do any harm.

"Do no harm," Connor said aloud. "I think she's a little late for that discussion."

The camera showed a photo of Kate, then a photo of Jeff along with the number for the tip hotline. The camera panned back to Candy, who told viewers that if they had seen or knew the whereabouts of either Kate or Jeff, they should call the number at the bottom of the screen. She then read the number for the TV viewers.

Connor glanced around his and Kate's office. It had become a war room of sorts. There were maps with colored pushpins. Red pins were positive, confirmed sightings. Blue pins were sightings too vague to confirm.

The elevator chimed. Deputy David Smith walked in and headed straight for Connor's desk. "I have something for you," Deputy Smith said, tossing an offense/incident report on Connor's desk.

Connor set down his coffee cup. "A wreck? Deputy, I don't do accidents. You need to see the patrol division downstairs."

"This isn't just any wreck, Detective." Deputy Smith opened the report, turned it toward Connor, and pointed at the name. Connor saw "Jeff Gilbert" and quickly sat forward.

"The Hampton murder happened that same night, within about thirty minutes of this wreck. I saw his photo on the BOLO and knew I recognized the name and the face. It took me a minute to put it all together. Then I had to pull the reports. He wasn't in the clothes you mentioned in your report, but he could have changed." Deputy Smith pulled up a chair, waiting for Connor's response.

"Once he got in the wreck, he must have chosen this place as his dumping ground. We found IDs as well as other things out there," Connor said, looking over the full report.

"Isn't this also where he abducted Detective Stroup?" Deputy Smith inquired.

"Yes." Connor looked across at the empty desk and chair where Kate usually sat. "Yes, it is."

"How the hell did he overpower her?" Deputy Smith asked.

"We don't know. She never should've gone out there alone in the first place. The caller told her it was his attorney's office wanting to clear up some details. I assume she thought she was simply going out there to meet with his attorney or an assistant."

A call coming in on his desk phone interrupted Connor. He signaled to the deputy to wait as he took the call.

"What! Why in the H-E-L-L didn't they report this sooner?" Connor raised his voice as he slammed down the receiver and shook his head.

Rubbing his hand through the stubble on his face, Connor stood, walked over to the white board, and pulled Ellie's photo off it. He quickly made a copy and handed it to Deputy Smith.

"What's this?"

Connor grabbed his sport coat. "The vic's girlfriend is missing. They think since the same day Kate turned up missing," Connor said, heading toward the elevator.

Sundae and Deputy Smith followed him.

As the men entered the elevator, Smith asked, "You think he has both women?"

"Her parents live out of town. When they reported Ellie missing, they said she calls them every day. The last call was two days ago. They called her workplace and were told she hadn't been in or called in for two days. You do the math, Deputy. Have your deputies look for her, too. Oh, and thank you for the copy of the report."

Connor quickly stopped at the dispatcher's desk and handed the photo to the dispatcher.

"After you do a BOLO on her, would you have someone put the photo back on my desk? Her physical details are in my initial reports. Also let the Hampton family know. They live out of state. Request a welfare check on them from the local PD and ask the PD to place a car at their house if they can, in case this maggot has really slipped a cog. I'll be heading to Ellie's house."

Deputy Smith stopped Connor. "Do you think

the girlfriend and Gilbert could be working this thing together?"

"In this line of work, I've learned to never discount anything."

Connor started through the door, then turned back to the dispatcher. "Also, please try calling Beth Ellis. I've been trying to reach her since…" Connor stopped and thought to himself. Surely Gilbert couldn't have been brazen enough to take three women. Then he remembered that this was the same man who had walked into a house with three people in it and killed the victim, execution style, in his bed.

"Just please call the profiler and ask her to call me ASAP!"

CHAPTER 27

Connor, Sundae, and Detectives Barton and Harris found the back door to Ellie's home unlocked and open. They saw signs of a struggle. Two chairs in the kitchen had been overturned. Droplets of blood dotted the floor and the side of the white kitchen cabinet. Ellie had put up a fight – or so it appeared.

Connor quickly called dispatch to have them check on Ellie's daughter. When dispatch called back to say that Ellie's daughter was safely with her father, Sam Peters, Connor requested a uniformed patrol by the Peters' house. Dispatch conveyed to Connor that Ellie had called her daughter each evening when the daughter had visitation with her father, but had not done so the last two days. Sam had thought it odd, but he didn't bother to call anyone. Also, dispatch said to let Connor know that they had made contact with Beth Ellis, the profiler, and that she was okay.

"Have there been any demands?" Bob asked.

"Nothing." Connor sat, thinking while surveying the kitchen. "You said that when you and Grant went to the Gilbert office, Jeff's car was parked in the employee parking lot, but he wasn't there, right?"

"That's correct," Bob said.

"Did you ask if any of the company vehicles were missing?"

"Already checked. Everything was accounted for," Grant said.

Connor reached for his phone and called dispatch on speaker.

"Can you check on whether any rental cars, vans, or trucks were reported missing on the day of the abductions?" Connor asked.

Sandy looked through her logs for the date. "Nothing," she replied regretfully. "But let me..." She looked at the following day's entries, then saw it. "Wait. The day after the abduction, an SUV wasn't returned. Patrol unit 55 found it on the outskirts of town."

"Where?" Connor asked.

Sandy read the location. "Ninety-Eighth Street."

"Ninety-Eighth. Isn't that where Warehouse Row is?"

Warehouse Row was the nickname the officers had given the area. There was row upon row of warehouses, some in use and others abandoned and boarded up.

"Sandy, send me the rental car company's contact info. They may have video from when the SUV was leased. We'd be able to see who leased it. Has the patrol officer submitted his report on the SUV he found?"

The line was silent. Then Sandy came back on. "No, he hasn't turned in the report and officer 55 is off duty today."

All three detectives shook their heads.

"Call his cell phone. We need any info he has on this, ASAP! Oh, Sandy, thank you."

Seconds later, Connor received a text from Sandy with the contact information for the rental car location.

"I'm going over to the rental car place. Would

you two go back to the Gilberts' business and find out if they have a warehouse in Warehouse Row? Maybe that's where he's holding the women," Connor said.

"We'll lock this up," said Grant as Connor headed out to the rental car business.

Connor looked at his watch. It was getting close to five, and he didn't know whether anyone would be there to look up past rentals after that time. He rushed through traffic.

"Welcome to Easy Rentals. I'll be right with you," the agent said with a big smile.

Connor removed his badge from his belt. "Lakewood Police. I need to know if you can look up who rented the SUV that was abandoned the day after its rental."

The lady at the head of the line let out an audible sigh and gave Connor a disgusted look. "Honey, he said he'll be right with you," the woman said.

"I heard him."

The agent glanced back and forth between Connor and the woman as though he were watching a tennis match.

"Is that a service dog?" The lady looked at Sundae and pointed.

The hair on Sundae's back stood up and she growled at the woman.

"Lady, honestly…"

The agent interrupted Connor. "You'll have to go to our office on 6th Street. That's where we keep all our rental records, Officer." The agent turned his attention back to the anxious lady in line.

Connor turned and left, looking at his wristwatch. He should have asked the agent for their office hours; however, the rude customer had really gotten under his skin. Once again, Connor weaved in and out of traffic, making every attempt to get there before 5:00.

"You didn't like that woman very much either, did you Sundae?" Connor chuckled, knowing that Sundae had simply been giving a warning when the woman had suddenly raised her hand.

Connor pulled into the driveway of Easy Rentals on 6th at exactly 4:55. He ran to the door and pulled on the handle, but the door refused to open. He looked down and saw the gold leaf lettering on the glass door: "Hours of operation, 9:00 to 4:00." Connor ran to the back of the building, praying that someone was working late. The parking lot was as empty as a toy store's shelves on Christmas Eve.

Connor walked back to his car. The first twenty-four hours of any kidnapping were the most important. It was now forty-eight hours without any contact or demands. What kind of monster was Jeff Gilbert and what was he capable of doing?

CHAPTER 28

The windows were clouded with a coating that consisted of years of age, dirt, and weather. They resembled the frosted glass of a shower stall more than they did safety glass, as one could barely make out the wire mesh embedded into the safety panels. Nonetheless, Jeff could tell it was still daylight because he knew the panels became black at night.

His hair was dirty and in disarray. He hadn't shaved in the past two days and he kept rubbing the stubble on his face, as he was not used to having facial hair. He paced the large building like a madman, back and forth.

Why didn't Ellie like him? He couldn't understand. What had she seen in Bud Hampton?

Even with Bud out of the way, she wanted nothing to do with him. She had glared at him with hostility and anger when he'd showed up at her door. He'd had to take her forcefully from her house. If only Bud hadn't gotten in their way, he wouldn't have had to do what he did that night. Nor would he have done what he did the other day. It was all Bud's fault. The thought made him angrier.

"No!" Jeff yelled like a crazy man. He had to put the rest of his plan into action. Now it was time to make contact with the Lakewood Police Department. He had made them wait long enough.

Jeff assured himself that he was in control. Once he completed his plan, Ellie would have no choice but to love him. Bud was dead and Brad had lost his career when he had become the focus of a murder investigation. Besides, he had another girlfriend, but that wouldn't matter. Tonight, he and Ellie would be jetting across the ocean.

Connor was sitting at his desk, waiting for a call from Barton and Harris, when his phone rang.

"Maxwell," Connor answered as he picked up the handset.

It was Sandy, the dispatcher.

"Connor, first I want to let you know that the FBI is here and they and our guys are already tracing this call." She paused, then continued."I think this may be the call you've been waiting for… Jeff Gilbert."

"Put him on."

The line was silent for a few seconds. "Sir, go ahead. I have Detective Maxwell on the line for you," Sandy said, then disconnected her line.

"Detective Maxwell, it seems I have what you're looking for."

There was silence on the phone. Connor knew the longer he could keep Jeff on the line, the better the chance that they could trace where the call was coming from.

"Looking for…who is this?" Connor played dumb. The elevator chimed as Bob Barton and Grant Harris walked in. Connor motioned for them to be quiet and to pick up the other line to listen in.

"Don't play stupid with me, Detective. You know I have your little companion cop. I have to say, she's quite pretty, too."

Connor looked at the wall clock. He wrote a note asking Detective Harris to find out if the FBI and IT people had a location on this SOB yet. Harris jumped up and left the room.

"I want to talk to her," Connor demanded.

"I'm sure you do," Jeff said as he chuckled. "That simply isn't going to happen." Jeff felt the power and control.

Harris returned to the room with a printed note. "Feds are here; they have their equipment on the line with our guys, nothing yet."

Connor shrugged his shoulders as if to ask why. Harris just shook his head.

"So, here's what I want. Got a paper, Detective? I don't want you to forget any of this." Jeff wiped the sweat from his face.

"Go ahead...Jeff, what is it you want?"

Jeff began pacing again. He hadn't taken any of his antipsychotic medication in two days and he was becoming edgier.

"I want three million dollars from my dad. All one-hundred-dollar bills. No consecutive or marked bills. I want my dad's private jet and pilot. Is that understood? I want all this by tonight."

Jeff was sweating profusely now. His arms became more animated as he spoke. "I'm waiting, Detective."

"Jeff, we need time to get in touch with your

dad. Plus, the banks are all closed by now. There's no way…"

Connor was interrupted by Jeff's angry outburst. "You stupid cop! All of you are dumb, dumb, dumb! I know the banks are closed. My dad has that much and more in the home safe."

Connor raised his eyebrows at Bob. Both men were thinking, 'Who keeps that much money in a home safe?'

"Jeff, we need you to guarantee that if we do what you want, we'll get Kate and Ellie back safely," Connor said.

"You'll get Kate back. Not Ellie. She's mine! Does your little cop brain understand that?"

Connor looked over at Harris, who was on the phone across the room. In large letters, Connor wrote, "Do they have anything?"

Harris shook his head no.

"I understand, Jeff. Just tell me where and when."

"Take a taxi to my father's private hangar at the Lakewood airport. I want your cop dog to bring me the money. Is that understood?" Jeff demanded.

"Jeff, my beagle couldn't carry that much money."

"So have it drag the money. Put it in a damn

wagon if you have to. If any cops show up, the mutt gets it first, then the lady cop. Eight o'clock tonight."

Jeff disconnected the call and smiled. He knew by that night, he and Ellie would be on their honeymoon far, far away from Lakewood. Far from her ex-husband and that kid of theirs.

"Call the Gilberts. Tell them Jeff's demands and see if we can put this all together in…" Connor looked at the wall clock. "Two hours." Getting up, he headed to the elevator.

"Where are you going?" Bob asked.

"Downstairs to the FBI and our IT guys. I want to see if they're using two tin cans and string to trace this call."

Connor burst into the IT department and found more men in black or blue suits than Macy's had on their racks.

"What the…" Connor said as one of the men in a black suit grabbed him by the arm.

"Detective, I understand you're all under stress here," FBI Agent Young said. "We did everything possible, but that call was bounced off not one but twenty cell towers. There was no way we could trace the call. Whoever this guy is, he either knows phone systems or paid someone to do that."

CHAPTER 29

Connor walked back into the squad room with Agent Young and introduced him to both Barton and Harris.

"Connor, we didn't have a chance to tell you that the Gilberts weren't home. We waited there for an hour to find out about the warehouse. No one showed up," said Bob, knowing this was going to add even more stress to the situation.

"We can assume Jeff knows what his dad's pilot looks like. I have my men in touch with your people. Because he's a licensed pilot, we can find out who he is. I need all the intel you've gathered on the Gilberts so I can have my people locate them," Agent Young said.

Connor grabbed the file and dug through it until

he found the paperwork. He handed it over to
Agent Young, who took it and calmly headed for the
elevator.

"Do their mommies always dress them the
same?" Harris joked.

The joke went right over Connor's head.

"Well, gentlemen, let's go downstairs and see if
they're able to find the Gilberts," Connor said as the
three detectives and Sundae headed for the elevator.

Connor looked at his watch. The time was 7:55 p.m.
He sat in the backseat of the taxi with Sundae. The
cab driver had been replaced with an FBI agent
dressed in a plaid shirt and worn jeans. Connor had
practiced unsuccessfully with Sundae, having her
drag weights – sixty-six pounds – inside a bag.
Sundae weighed only twenty pounds, and that was
with her collar and badge. Then they moved the
weights over to a rolling duffle bag. Sundae still
struggled to drag the duffle because it had only
wheels on the back and was lying flat.

One of the IT people watched the poor little
beagle struggling and suddenly got an idea. He
grabbed an electronic equipment dolly, quickly

removed its two wheels and axle, and placed them on the front of the bag. The bag could lay flat and hopefully Sundae would be able to drag it to the jet.

They stood back as Connor gave the command to drag. This time, Sundae was able to pull the blue duffle bag with the sixty-six pounds of weight inside it.

Jeff had said that once he had the money and the pilot, he would release Kate. Then, off he and Ellie would go to an undisclosed destination. After that, the pilot would fly back home. However, the FBI had its own plan.

As soon as the call from Jeff ended, the FBI deployed a team of marksmen with night sights to the rooftops on and around the Gilberts' hangar. Each marksman had a lookout man with binoculars equipped to see at night. Additional men and women were placed around the Gilberts' hangar. The idea was that this would allow the team to take the very best positions long before Jeff got there. Their hope was that Jeff himself would step out to get the money long enough to give the team a good shot. The pilot knew the risks but as an ex-military man, he felt he could handle whatever came his way. He was also to give a note to Jeff, written by Mrs. Gilbert, begging her son to give up his plan.

The tarmac was dark except for several security lights around the hangar and the blinking lights of the runways in the distance. The Feds had closed the runways down until the issue was resolved.

Once the pilot pushed the jet out of the hangar with the aid of an aircraft tug, he gave a code signaling that Jeff was on board. No one, including the FBI, knew when or how he had gotten there, or if the two women were with him on the jet.

"You ready for this? I just got word that he's already on board," said the FBI agent driving the taxi.

"How did he get into the jet…unless he was holed up inside the hangar all this time?" Connor said.

The FBI agent stopped the taxi about a hundred and fifty yards from the jet. Connor felt beads of sweat rolling down his chest as he got out of the taxi on the opposite side of the car. His cellphone rang. The FBI knew Jeff might try to make contact with Connor and could hear both sides of the conversation.

"I told you, just the mutt. I'll kill her and the mutt," Jeff screamed into the phone, his hands were shaking.

"Jeff, I had to put the money in a duffle bag. The

dog can't open the trunk of a car," Connor said as he pulled the blue bag out of the trunk and sat it on the runway. Pulling Sundae close to him, he hugged her. He whispered, "I love you, Sundae, be safe."

He handed the leather leash to Sundae and pointed toward the jet. Sundae began dragging the bag slowly toward the jet as practiced.

"Jeff, the dog can't drag the bag up the stairs. You'll have to come get it," Connor said.

"I'm sure you and your friends would love that, wouldn't you?" Jeff laughed manically. "No way in hell will I allow that."

Connor commanded Sundae to stop. She quickly stopped and sat next to the bag. "So, how is the dog supposed to get the money to you?" Connor asked.

"You'll see soon enough."

Connor gave the command to start dragging the money. Slowly, the little beagle pulled the duffle bag across the tarmac. Once she had reached the foot of the stairway to the jet, Jeff called Connor.

"Command her to unzip the bag," Jeff demanded.

This wasn't something Connor had planned on, or something for which he had trained Sundae. He thought for a second. Sundae knew how to search for drugs, but would she do the open technique without the scent of drugs in the bag – with only his command?

"Jeff, I'm really not sure if she knows how to do this," Connor said.

"The mutt does it or I have a bead on her right now."

"Jeff, I told you, if anyone – including my dog – gets hurt, that jet will never take flight. Do you understand me?" Connor angrily said.

"I don't think you understand, Detective. I hold all the cards in this game."

"I need to get closer to Sundae to give the command." Connor knew he was adding another playing card to Jeff's hand, adding his own life into the equation. Connor didn't wait for a reply; he started walking with his hands up. Agent Young, in a command center van, shook his head no.

"No, Connor!" Agent Young said, which echoed in Connor's earpiece.

"Sundae, drop the leash," Connor commanded. Sundae dropped the leather leash from her mouth and looked at Connor.

"Good girl!" Connor praised Sundae as she sat next to the bag.

"Sundae, inside," Connor commanded. He was

five feet away from Sundae. From this vantage point, he could see that Jeff had the gun pointed at him. However, there was no sign of the two women. Connor wiped the sweat from his forehead.

"Don't come any closer!" Jeff demanded.

Sundae tilted her head back and forth, which was her signal to Connor that she didn't understand his command. She didn't sense any drugs inside the bag she had just dragged more than one hundred yards.

"Sundae, inside!" Connor commanded again, this time motioning toward the bag.

Sundae moved toward the zipper and put her two front paws on the bag. She leaned down and pulled the zipper about three inches. Then she looked at Connor.

"That's enough," Jeff said. He moved a few steps away to the opposite side of the jet so that he could get a better look at the bag's contents.

"Agent Young, I have a bead on the suspect," said one of the marksmen. This meant he felt certain he could take the shot.

"Don't take it. He'll kill the detective and probably the dog."

"Jeff, send Kate out now. The money is all here," Connor demanded.

While Jeff was fixated on watching Connor and Sundae, Kate silently wiggled her hands free, and then undid her feet. Ellie watched in horror, as Kate got up free; she feared what Jeff would do to Kate or her. He was crazy and out of touch with reality; God knows what he would do.

Jeff pointed the Glock and leveled it at Connor. As he was about to take a shot, Kate rushed forward. Startled, Jeff turned as his gun discharged a bullet, hitting Kate in the chest. The marksman tried to stay on his mark just as Sundae bolted at lightning speed up the jet's steps. She lunged at Jeff and her teeth ripped into his gun hand.

Connor ran up the steps two at a time, his gun drawn and his heart pounding. Stopping, he squeezed the trigger just as the FBI marksman was finally able to take his shot. A crack echoed through the darkness as three shots were fired, followed by deafening silence.

CHAPTER 30

*C*onnor sat, silently watching the rain run down the large windowpane in long streaks. In the darkened room, the windows reflected the medical monitors and equipment attached to Kate. It was almost like Connor was simply watching a TV show. Nonetheless, the pumping sound of the respirator and the beeping of the monitors in the room always brought him back to the reality that Kate's life was hanging by a thread.

Was it one, maybe two…no, three days he had sat by her hospital bed? He had lost track of time. He ate only when someone brought him something. He wanted to be there when she woke up. IF she woke up. The doctors hadn't given him much hope after the surgery to remove the bullet that had lodged itself dangerously close to her spine after passing through her chest. They told him she had lost a lot of blood.

He recalled running up the steps after the FBI sniper had killed Jeff. Connor had sat on the floor, holding Kate, trying to stop the bleeding until the EMT took over. Then he felt frozen in time as he watched the blinking lights of the ambulance that took her away. He remembered trying to reach for a pair of latex gloves in his pocket so that he could pick up the gun Jeff had used. This was a crime scene after all; it was second nature to him.

It was then that Agent Young put his arm on Connor's shoulder and told him they would take care of the scene. He remembered that at some point, someone had escorted Ellie from the back of the plane. She was crying when she put her arms around Connor.

As the parade of doctors, nurses, technicians, and respiratory specialists came in, the memories faded for a short time. After they left, Connor was left with the gruesome details of what had happened, what he had seen, heard, and felt. The worst part was that he was left with Kate in a coma.

What the hell was a coma, anyway? Connor

wondered, was it somewhere between heaven and earth? Was Kate caught between layers, waiting for God or her to decide if she lived or died? Only when his mind became thoroughly exhausted did he drift off to sleep.

While sleeping in the chair next to Kate's bed, he heard a soft knock at the door. In the hallway, Mr. and Mrs. Gilbert stood at the door to Kate's room. Connor shook the stiffness out of his legs and walked to the door.

"Detective Maxwell, we are truly sorry. We wanted to come by the day after, but…the guilt of what our son did has kept us away," Mrs. Gilbert said with tears in her eyes. She looked into Connor's eyes with compassion. "We wanted so much for our son. I should've noticed how his personality had changed over the last few years. I was busy and so was my husband."

"Detective, I think what my wife is trying to say is that we're very sorry and have made arrangements with the hospital to pay for all Detective Stroup's expenses here in the hospital and once she is released… "

Connor interrupted Mr. Gilbert. "You mean *if* she's released, don't you?"

Mr. Gilbert bowed his head. "I understand your anger, Detective, really I do."

"We were told Kate has been your partner for several years," Mrs. Gilbert said. "Please allow us to help in the only way we can. Our son is gone; there is nothing we can do for him. Kate may be out of work for weeks or months, or possibly never be able to work again. We will take care of all her bills."

Connor raised his hand to stop her. Mrs. Gilbert refused to stop talking.

"Detective Maxwell, we are well aware she may not make it. You don't have to remind us of the damage our son did. We care and wish there was some way we could've stopped him."

The Gilberts turned and left Connor standing in the hallway.

Bob and Grant came to visit Kate, bringing Sundae with them into her room. Sundae stood up with her front paws on the bed, looking at Kate. Then she turned and looked at Connor. He lifted her up and Sundae lay down carefully beside Kate. Connor picked up Kate's hand and put it on Sundae's back. He watched as canine and human somehow made a connection in the odd place called a coma. Kate looked as if she was smiling in her sleep.

"Connor, you need to get out of here and come back to work. Kate has all the help she needs," Grant said. Bob nodded in agreement.

Connor knew they were right. The sergeant had told him to take all the time he needed, but he was a lead detective for the Lakewood Police Department and had to get back to work.

"Maybe tomorrow," Connor said. He woke Sundae up and lifted her off the bed. Then he walked Bob and Grant out into the hallway.

"Connor, those two women were living in deplorable conditions. He had two large dog runs inside the hangar. That's how he contained them. Ellie told us he abducted her first and took her out to Highway 10. When Kate pulled her unit off the highway, Gilbert forced Ellie to scream for help. Kate ran into an ambush. She never stood a chance," Bob explained.

Connor shook his head, not saying a word.

"We better be going," Grant said.

Sundae turned and looked over her shoulder to see if Connor would follow. When he didn't, her tail dropped and she slowly walked away with Barton and Harris.

The following day, Connor left the hospital and

picked up Sundae. Each day after work, they went to the hospital to visit Kate. Connor would pick Sundae up and gently place her next to Kate. He then carefully put Kate's arm on Sundae's back. Sundae would drift off to sleep. Connor would tell Kate all about his day, even though she lie lifelessly in the hospital bed.

A nurse came in quietly. "You know, they say they can hear you when they're in a coma." She checked Kate's vitals, charted them, and gave Connor a hug on her way out of the room.

Connor thought about what the nurse had said. He wondered if Kate could really hear him, or if she knew that he was there with her and that Bob, Grant, and other members of the department had been there. Even some of the sheriff's deputies had come in.

He took her hand in his, looking at her. "Kate, please…Sundae and I need you," Connor said and kissed her on the cheek.

Carefully, he woke Sundae and lifted her off the bed. He stood there looking at Kate and ran his hand through her hair. Connor turned to leave, then quickly turned back. Did he just see what he thought he saw?

Watching Kate's face, he saw it again. Her

eyelids fluttered. He quickly pushed the call button and a nurse came in.

"Watch her eyes," Connor said to the nurse.

The nurse reached over and held Kate's hand. "Her hand has movement as well."

Connor felt his eyes tearing up. He reached down and picked up Sundae. Could this nightmare finally be over? Kate tried again and this time opened her eyes.

"Hi there, sweetie," the nurse said as Kate looked from Connor to the nurse. "Do you know where you are?"

Kate looked at the nurse, confused.

"You're at the Lakewood General Hospital," the nurse explained. "Do you know this man?" The nurse pointed at Connor. "And this dog?" The nurse waited.

As Kate looked at Connor and Sundae, a big smile crossed her face.

A MESSAGE FROM TIM

I hope you enjoyed this book; there are more to come. Book reviews are crucial, both for me as the author and for your fellow readers. Please take the time to leave a review at your favorite bookseller. I would greatly appreciate it.

Thank you,
Timothy Glass

ABOUT THE AUTHOR

 Timothy Glass was born in Pennsylvania but grew up in Central New Mexico. Tim graduated from the University of New Mexico. He later spent some time in New England and central Florida.

Glass is an award-winning author, illustrator, cartoonist, and writing instructor. Tim has worked as a ghostwriter and a story consultant. Glass started his writing career as a journalist under the pen name of C. Stewart. He has written and published more than 300 nonfiction articles nationally and internationally for the health and fitness industry. Glass worked as a regular contributing writer for several New York-based magazines.

Until the magazine's retirement in the late 1990's, Tim was a freelance journalist for It's a Wrap magazine, a New Mexico entertainment quarterly.

VISIT US ON THE WEB

Visit Tim's website at www.timglass.com. Also, don't forget to check out his beagle cartoons at http://www.timglass.com/ Cartoons/

Sign up for Tim's newsletter:
http://www.timglass.com/join.htm

Join Tim on his fan pages:

Facebook:
https://www.facebook.com/pages/Timothy-Glass/146746625258?ref=ts

Twitter: www.twitter.com/timothyglass/

LinkedIn: http://www.linkedin.com/in/ timothyglass

Check out our Sleepytown Beagles fabric and wrapping paper: https://www.spoonflower.com/profiles/ sleepytown_beagles

Join Tim on Pinterest: https://www.pinterest.com/timothyglas0417/

CPSIA information can be obtained
at www.ICGtesting.com
Printed in the USA
BVHW040711021118
531914BV00014B/13/P